THE CARIBBEA

CURSE OF THE BLACK AVENGER

EDDIE JONES

DRY BONES PUBLISHING

JUVENILE FICTION / ACTION
ADVENTURE / PIRATES

CURSE OF THE BLACK AVENGER

Copyright © 2019 by Eddie Jones

Jones, Eddie, 1957-

Curse of the Black Avenger / by Eddie Jones.

p. cm. — (Caribbean Chronicles ; book one)

Summary: "When fourteen-year-old Ricky Bradshaw has an absence seizure episode, he finds himself in the middle of a Caribbean pirate adventure.

If the sea spit you out, thrusting you back into the golden age of piracy, buried treasure and beauty beyond belief ... would you stay?" – Provided by publisher.

ISBN-13: 978-1-946016-70-6

[1. Pirates—Fiction. 2. Piracy—Fiction. 3. Humor—Fiction. 4. Fantasy and time travel.] I. Title.

Cover design: Elaina Lee
Interior design: atritex.com

Printed in the United States of America

CARIBBEAN CHRONICLES SERIES

BOOK ONE
CURSE OF THE BLACK AVENGER

BOOK TWO
DEAD CALM, BONE DRY

BOOK THREE
THE END OF CALICO JACK

Dedication

For Mason: the original Captain "Stinky" LaFoote.

I hope you enjoy *Curse of the Black Avenger*. If you do,
I would be grateful if you would write a brief review on
Amazon, Goodreads, or another bookseller's website. Love
it—hate it? Either way I would appreciate your comments.
Reviews are helpful to readers. Either way, thanks for
purchasing *Curse of the Black Avenger* and spending time
sailing with Ricky.

CONTENTS

Pirate Crew

Cast of Characters

RICKY

REBECCA

BARNACLE

CAPTAIN LaFOOTE

CHAPTER 1

BECKY NANCE

I had just ordered a large pizza the night our apartment building burned down.

Monday, it was. Christmas Eve. Pepperoni with extra cheese.

Becky Nance, a girl in my ninth-grade biology class, says cheese will give you zits, but it's not like a girl as pretty and popular as Becky is going to hang out with a nobody like me. Not with my pigeon-toed feet, lanky arms, and bony shoulders.

So I ordered a pizza. Then I went outside to meet the delivery guy.

No matter how many times I've ordered from Papa Ron Jon's Pizza the delivery guys can never find our apartment. The guy ends up walking all over the complex banging on doors until the pizza is as hard as a hubcap. You would think if he's a driver he would use GPS and Google Maps or something.

1

Mom does. But then Mom knows how important it is to make deliveries on time.

Mom is a truck driver. She had a load of video games that needed to be delivered to a big-box department store in Memphis. When I got back from the mall there was a note on my dresser saying she was sorry about missing Christmas and all, but it couldn't be helped. She promised to swing by Graceland and pick up a snow globe from the gift shop. I'm not what you would call a fan of Elvis but Mom's mom was, so Mom is. Besides, I like the snow globes Mom gets for me on her trips.

She had probably just pulled up to the loading dock of the department store when the fire in our apartment reached her bedroom.

Of course if I'd known our apartment was about to go up in flames I would have grabbed some stuff. Pictures of Dad, my basketball trophies, Mom's jewelry box, my seizure medication. Then again, if I'd bolted down the steps in a panic like everybody else on our floor I'd have probably tripped in the stairwell and made things worse.

That's been happening a lot, lately. Tripping, falling. I guess it's because I shot up six inches in the past year and now my feet catch on small things, like curbs and steps and the edge of the runner outside of our biology class. I hate the way my hands hang apelike by my sides, palms perspiring whenever Becky looks at me, which almost never happens. Becky has only spoken to me twice this year: once in biology when she made the comment about pizza and zits and then last day of classes before winter break when she summoned me to her lunch table. I had been sitting in an area of the cafeteria traditionally occupied by boys with hairless armpits, glasses, and no hope at all of penetrating the inner sanctuary of the Pretty and Popular Girls group.

So I hurried toward her table with a nervous palpitation in my chest.

Palpitation is one of the new words my English teacher, The Captain, put on our exam. The Captain is a large smelly man with yellow teeth, permanent sweat stains under his armpits, and an irrational dislike of me. He's always ordering me to sit still and be quiet, even though that's exactly what I do every day in his class. He's a former Marine drill sergeant, even though you would hardly know it because he wears his long, shaggy black hair in a ponytail. There's a single eyebrow growing across his forehead that looks like a giant caterpillar.

Approaching Becky's table I stifled the urge to blurt out, "Hey, Becky. I think you're hot. Want to catch a movie with me, sometime?" Instead what I said was, "'Sup?"

The look she gave me made it clear she had already figured out I was an idiot. "Roger, I need to ask you something."

"Ricky," I said. "My name is Ricky Bradshaw."

Becky rolled her eyes. Becky has pretty green eyes, even when they roll. "You sure your name's not Roger?"

"It's Ricky," I said, unnecessarily. "We have biology together?"

"Right. That's why I called you over. I wanted to ask if you could loan me your class notes over winter break. I've missed some days because of cheerleading practice. A bunch, actually. You have no idea how intense cheerleading competition can be."

She was right. I had no idea how intense cheerleading competition could be. But I was willing to find out.

"One of the girls in my class told me you take great notes," she said. "That you write down everything. Are you, like, artistic?"

"You mean autistic. And, no. It's just that I really have to focus on my grades. See, it's only my mom and me and we're not what you'd call rich, so if I'm going to go to college I need to—"

"I'm sort of in a hurry here, Rog. Can I get those study notes or not?"

My armpits began to sweat. The pizza-zits on my forehead felt like volcanic peaks preparing to erupt. *Becky Nance, talking to me. How cool is that?*

I said, "Give me your number and we'll meet up after school."

"I have a cheerleading event at the mall tonight, so if you could swing by basketball practice and drop them off with Ed, that'd be awesome. You know Ed? His dad owns a Porsche dealership?"

I know Ed. I hate Ed. "Backup point guard on JV, right?"

"Starting. And he was my escort on homecoming court."

"But I thought he missed the game?"

"Okay, he *would have been* my escort, except something came up."

"Went paintballing is what I heard."

"With his cousins."

"Only saying, if you'd asked me to be your date, I wouldn't have missed it for the world."

"Rog, if *you* had been my date to homecoming court, I would have shot *myself* with a paint gun."

After school I DID NOT drop off my class study notes with Ed as promised. Instead I caught a ride to the mall to get Mom a Christmas present. Becky and her team were doing cartwheels in front of a kiosk selling nail polish, eyelash threading, and false eyelashes. I asked Becky if she wanted to do something with me afterwards. Becky rolled her gorgeous green eyes and told me to "drop dead."

Turns out the next night that's exactly what happened.

CHAPTER 2

STUPID MICROWAVE

Here is how I sort of died. Christmas Eve night, the evening after I saw Becky at the mall, I was sitting on the couch watching the Wizards tank another game so they could move up in draft picks when Mom called. She had just reached the Memphis city limits.

"You eat yet?" she asked.

"Cooking popcorn. You going to be home in time for breakfast?"

Mom always cooks eggs, grits, biscuits, and bacon on Christmas morning. She also gets me a big thing of chocolate milk and lets me drink all I want.

"Sorry, Ricky. Traffic was just awful coming around Nashville and I lost my slot at the loading dock. I'm hoping to get unloaded any minute. I got you a neat present."

"It's another snow globe, isn't it?"

"Why say it like that?"

"It's fine, Mom. Really. I can never have too many."

"Be careful with the microwave."

"I will."

"Remember the timer doesn't work."

"I know."

"And don't put too much salt on it. You know what the doctor said about how salt can trigger an episode."

Mom said this as if I didn't know that I suffer from absence seizures. Like I'd forgotten that I have epilepsy and can sometimes zone out for a few seconds.

"I won't."

"I fixed you supper. It's in your bedroom." I walked into my bedroom. Dinner was a twenty-dollar bill with a coupon for two dollars off a large pepperoni pizza. "If you go out for any reason, and I hope you do not, don't forget to set the dead bolt. You forgot last time. And no company."

"Mom, it's Christmas Eve. All my friends are home with *their* families."

"Please don't say that, Ricky. You know I'd rather be there with you than parked here on the side of this highway waiting for my dispatcher to call."

"I better go so I can call in my order. No telling how long it'll take the pizza guy."

"Love you, Ricky. We'll open presents tomorrow."

"Mom?"

"Yes?"

"If you see Elvis, tell him I said 'hi.'"

I grabbed my coat and went outside to wait for the driver.

I stood at the end of our parking lot wearing a thick wool overcoat, my favorite Ron Jon surf shirt (which is why I always order pizza from the same place even though they can't find our apartment), jeans, and sneakers. Heavy snowflakes swirled around streetlights. A cold wind blew in from the Chesapeake Bay and up the creek. Across the street at the public docks a halyard slapped the metal mast of a sailboat. I had been

6

standing there for maybe ten minutes when the delivery driver swung into the first drive of our complex. Of course he parked in front of the wrong building.

Right about after I finished paying for my pizza I heard the goose-honk of a fire truck's horn. Looking up at our unit I saw the drapes of the patio's sliding glass door burst into flames. Seconds later the glass doors blew. *The popcorn in the microwave!*

The fire spread fast. Flames licked tree branches, melting the snow. Black smoke poured out windows. The swirl of flashing red lights illuminated snow-capped pine tops. I don't know how you would react if you had burned down a building by accident on Christmas Eve and watched as your neighbors huddled together on the grass median between the two parking lots, but I ran.

Actually, I walked across the street to the docks. The crowd in front of my apartment building spilled into the street, driven back by the heat. The curious drove by, gawking at the blaze. A man in a pickup truck pulled to where I was standing in front of the marina parking lot, rolled down his window, and said, "Any idea how it started?"

I shook my head. To be honest, I wasn't one hundred percent sure the fire was my fault. Maybe it was the microwave. Or maybe a strand of Christmas tree lights sparked. Maybe a candle tipped over. Last winter, someone had tried to refill a kerosene heater without waiting for it to cool and the thing exploded.

I carried my cold hard-as-a-hubcap pizza across the marina parking lot and the docks. Behind me police cruisers arrived; a television van unlimbered a rooftop boom and bathed the building in lights.

I looked up at the *Pride of Virginia*. The *Pride of Virginia* is a replica of an old sailing vessel from, like, a gazillion years ago. During the spring and summer, her crew offers day-sails and sunset tours to tourists willing to plunk down fifty dollars. I stood on the dock and listened as the wind howled through the *Pride's* rigging. Here's a drawing of me looking out my window at the *Pride of Virginia*.

The edge of furled sails fluttered beneath wooden spreaders. Hoping no one was looking, I stepped aboard and peered through a large port window. Below was a narrow passageway that led into a large cabin. Rows of bunks lined both sides of the huge room. Amidships, just aft of the mast, stood a long dining table. Small wooden barrels served as stools.

All the doors were locked, of course, so I ducked behind the deckhouse. Brushing away snow, I sat with my back braced against the small, wooden door, eating my cold pizza. That's when the stupid dog showed up begging for a slice of my pizza. Long, tangled fur. Floppy ears, curly tail.

He lifted one paw; I chewed.

He wagged his tail; I chewed some more.

He barked.

I hate a dog that begs by barking. I gave him a slice. "One piece, that's all you get."

I said this mostly for my benefit; the dog couldn't understand me. Some people talk to their dog like it's a person. But it's not a person. It's a dog.

And this dog definitely did not understand because he took the whole pizza, box and all.

By the time I reached the gangplank he was halfway up the dock and heading for the parking lot.

"Drop it!"

To my surprise, the mangy mutt did just that.

Backing away, he sat on his haunch. I eyed my pizza, which was now covered in dog slobber and fur and a little bit of snow.

"Stupid dog." I dropkicked the pizza and box into the water. Okay, fine me for littering. I was ticked. "Stupid dog," I said again to the dog that couldn't understand me.

What I'm about to tell you shows just how stupid that dog was. The mutt jumped into the freezing cold creek and swam after the soggy pizza that was floating away. You hear about how some dogs are good swimmers. Labs, for instance. And Chesapeake Bay retrievers. This dumb dog wasn't that sort of breed. This mutt had trouble keeping his head above water.

Small waves began to break over his head. He began lifting his front paws high like a Clydesdale horse and trying to swim back to the dock. Seeing him kick like that made me feel a little sorry for him.

But only a little.

At the end of the dock I dropped to my knees and leaned out, both arms extended out. "Come on, boy. This way. Swim to me."

I looked around for a boat hook or life ring. Anything I could use to hook him.

He was fighting the current and getting closer, but not so close I could reach him. The top half of my body hung over the water. My tee shirt was soaked through from the ice and snow I was laying on.

"Come on, boy. You can do it."

Cold spray from waves splashed my cheeks. The dog's frantic panting blew mist into the air.

Then I smelled burning. But it wasn't burning like from wood and stuff. This was more like an electrical fire. And I knew what would come next.

The smell of burning wires always leads to tingling in my arms and legs, numbness in my hands, followed by me staring blankly ahead without really knowing what's going on around me. Usually this only lasts for a few seconds. If you didn't know I was having a seizure you would think I was daydreaming. If you've never heard of absence seizures, that's okay. A lot of people haven't. My teachers are a lot of those people.

So there I was lying on the dock with half my body hanging over the water, soaking wet and cold, and knowing I was about to mentally check out for a few seconds when I grabbed the dog by the fur on his neck.

And fell in.

CHAPTER 3

THE OLD MAN

When I surfaced and reached my hand up to grab the dock, the dock wasn't a dock. The dock was a raft floating in the water.

And it wasn't dark.

Or snowing.

Or cold.

A slit of blue sky slanted downward. Gulls circled. Above me a bright, hot sun seared my skin.

Tossing the dog onto wooden planks, I followed, flopping onto a rickety, poorly built raft that looked eerily similar to the dock I'd been on moments earlier. Only, like I said, the dock was a raft, now.

Here's the weird part: I knew I was having an absence seizure. And that had never happened before. Before when I had an episode I didn't know I was having an episode. But I knew I had to be having an episode because I'd lost my Ron Jon shirt and my jeans were cropped off above the knees. Coat and sneakers were gone.

In the distance I spied a sailing skiff slicing across the sea. Its single white sail fluttered with the irregular wave of a bed sheet clipped to a clothesline. An old man stood in the stern. He wore a wide straw hat, no shirt, and a brown smock around his waist. With his left hand he held the tiller, carefully guiding the sailing skiff over oily swells. I thought about waving to the man in the skiff but to be honest, all that work trying to save the stupid dog from drowning and being on the dock with it snowing and cold had left me exhausted. So I lay back, closed my eyes, and let the sun warm me.

Here's a drawing of me on the raft.

"¿Está bien?"

The old fisherman stood over me, his straw hat pushed back on his head. He had a deeply seamed face, tired brown eyes, and gray whiskers. He had also moved me from the raft into his sailing skiff.

"Como te llamas?"

I know a little Spanish, not much. I told him my name.

"You speak English, no." By *no*, he meant *yes*. "Fortunate you are I came along. Deez waters … day can be dangerous, no?"

I felt along the inside of my forearm and fingered the moist edge of a ragged flap of skin. Apparently I'd cut myself pretty bad on the dock piling's barnacles. The old man dipped a wooden bucket over the side, lifted it out, and splashed water on the gash. The sharp pain nearly bucked me off the skiff. He dipped the bucket again and soaked the wound a second time. The salt water burned. When he dipped the pail a third time, I grabbed his wrist. "Enough."

He emptied the bucket back into the sea, turned it upside down, and sat. His large feet looked like a pair of buckskin flippers. I was on my back, a smelly fishing net for a pillow. Overhead, high wispy clouds scudded past against blue sky. Water gurgled near my ear, just beyond the wooden slats of the boat's sides.

The old man pivoted on his bucket, reached behind, and produced a small pouch. Inside were a long, curved needle and a bolt of white thread. I'm not a fan of needles. Especially long, curved ones that look like they could reach into my chest and pull out a lung.

"For de main," he explained, cutting his eyes upward toward the large sail.

I know a few sail names from reading pirate books. Mizzen, jib, genoa, and Yankee. The main was the big one on the boom. I saw that it had been stitched to the point where patches made up the better part of the sail. Without a word, he pinched the skin around the gash and jabbed the needle in, pulling the thread through. I gritted my teeth.

After a few more pricks and pulls, he looked past me toward the horizon and frowned. "Los bandidos del mar. We must hurry."

I rose onto my elbows. In the distance, far beyond the oily swells, a black ship appeared on the horizon. "Pirates?"

He nodded solemnly. "Los bandidos del mar rule deez waters." Dropping the needle and thread back into the pouch, he wiped his forehead with the back of his hand. "We must be fast, no?" Pulling the mainsheet (rope that controls the mainsail), he brought the boom over the center of the skiff. The sail flattened; our speed increased.

"If they're really pirates like you say, will we be able to outrun them?"

He shrugged. His reaction did not encourage me.

Tying off the mainsheet, he gestured toward a line of breaking waves a mile or more ahead. I saw what he meant to do: sail through a ribbon of flat calm water slicing through the reef, one so narrow the captain of a big ship would not dare try.

From the stern of the skiff came whimpering. The old man reached back and placed the mangy mutt in his lap. "Was with you, no?"

"Not with me. Not sure whose dog it is, but it's not mine. Ask him."

In a guttural, coughing sound, the old man spoke to the dog in a way that sounded as if he were hocking up a fur ball. The dog's ears perked up. It cocked its head as if it understood—which, of course, it could not. The old man hacked and growled some more. The dog barked excitedly, then jumped from the old man's lap and burrowed under the fishing net.

"He no remember how he got here."

"Like you really understood what he was saying."

"Dogs, si. Cats, no. Cats they ... how you say ... boogie?"

"Snotty?"

"Si, snotty ease cats." Picking a piece of dried fish from the net, he tossed it toward the mutt. "He say ease name is Barnacle. Named after ease dad, Oyster. Ease your papa's dog, yes?"

"Dad is dead. Died when I was a toddler."

"Perhaps it ease as you say. Only dare ease dis man, we sailed together a long time ago. Your eyes, ease like his, yes?"

"Couldn't have been my dad. My father drove his rig into a bridge outside of Pittsburgh. Hit a patch of black ice and lost control."

"But he ease a sailor like you, no?"

"Dad? No way. Far as I know Dad never stepped foot on a boat."

Reaching into his pouch he rooted around. "May I show you something, Señor Ricky Bradshaw?" For a moment I was afraid he might pull out the needle and thread and stitch my eyebrows. Instead he held up a necklace with a gold pendant shaped like a ship's wheel. Turning it over, he pointed to the name on the back of the pendant. RICHARD JUSTICE BRADSHAW.

You read in books all the time about how someone's *heart leapt*. It's a cliché: the sort of phrase that hardly means anything because it's used so often. But my heart actually thumped against my rib cage and began quivering like a small animal trying to claw its way out of my chest.

"Ease your papa's." He handed me the pendant.

I studied its ship's wheel with twelve spokes. "Couldn't have been Dad's. Like I said, he's dead. But thanks, anyway. It's pretty cool looking."

"Do you think it is by chance I find you, Señor Ricky? Oh no. For a long time have I been sailing deez waters searching for a boy like you. One brave and smart in de ways of men. But we can discuss deez matters later. Right now you must decide if you will fight or flee?"

"Flee from what? That pirate ship?"

He scanned the water behind us, straining to see toward the horizon. The black ship had gained considerable ground, its sails clearly visible. "Los bandidos, yes, flee them we must. But you must also decide if you will stay here on dis sea among deez islands where dare is buried treasure and beauty beyond belief."

There did not seem to be much in the way of weapons in the sailing skiff. Fishing net. Harpoon. Ropes and scraps of canvas. "Fight with what?"

"Very well. Flee it is. But we must hope los bandidos do not know why you are here."

"How could they possibly know why I'm here? I don't even know where here is."

But as I was about to find out, *here* was in the middle of the Caribbean Sea during the golden age of piracy, where there was, in fact, buried treasure and beauty beyond belief waiting for those who could survive the curse of the *Black Avenger*.

CHAPTER 4

FIGHT OR FLEE

The old man thrust a spyglass into my hand. "Sight her flag."

That was sailor talk for "find out what sort of crew is chasing us: Spanish, French, Dutch, or English." No flag most likely meant pirates. I remembered from my reading about Blackbeard and Captain Kidd that pirates would often wait until they could spot the flag of the approaching vessel before hoisting their pirate flag. In this way they could draw close to the *prize* without suspicion.

"Turn that —"

"I know how it works," I interrupted, dialing in the focus on the spyglass.

On my fourteenth birthday I had received a cheap imitation spyglass from "Uncle Uncle," a bald, no-neck man with very big, very hairy forearms. Uncle Uncle was a call center rep for a telemarketing firm based out of Norfolk, Virginia and a semiprofessional kickboxer whose ringside tactics, in addition to breaking bones, gouging eyes, and spilling blood, often caused other competitors to give up soon after the bout's opening bell. Hence, the name "Uncle."

Of course Uncle Uncle wasn't my uncle at all. At the time he was only Mom's latest boyfriend, a thing that annoyed me to no end since, A) Dad was dead, and B) every time Uncle Uncle came over *I* had to sleep on the couch. We all pretended Uncle Joe was sleeping in my bed, but we also all knew this was not true. I would get up to go the bathroom in the middle of the night and hear him snoring in Mom's bedroom.

For my fourteenth birthday Uncle Uncle gave me an official "Master of the High Seas" spyglass, one of several in the "Commander" series. It was black, plastic, and made in China. Uncle Uncle seemed particularly pleased that he'd remembered my love for sailing and given me a gift to match. (Like he hadn't noticed the model clipper ships and pirate books, or nautical charts tacked to the ceiling over my room.)

The old man's spyglass gave me a sense of importance, as if I really *were* sailing the high seas. Except I was in a small, wooden skiff with a crazy man who claimed he'd sailed with my dead father. The heaviness of it reminded me of my first telescope; its brass tubing was worn dull from use. A black ring separated each section. When the scope was fully extended it nearly reached the length of my arm. I brought the small end to my eye and tried to sight the ship. Three masts, all draped with dark-colored sails. Men scurried about the deck. With each wave that slammed into the advancing ship its bow sent a froth of white spray high into the air.

"No flag," I said.

The old man's gaze fell. For a moment I thought he might be praying—or contemplating cutting his curled, yellow toenails.

Seconds passed before he said, "Bring out de long guns, dey will. If in a friendly mood, no?"

"And if they're not in a friendly mood?"

He placed his hand on my shoulder. "Pray you have the luck of your papa." Motioning toward a rope lying at my feet, he ordered me to "sheet in the jib." When I did, the skiff picked up another knot in speed.

For several minutes we sailed toward the breaking surf that crashed onto the reef. I began to think we might reach the calm-water channel when a shot whistled past overhead. The ball splashed into the water a few yards ahead, soaking us in its spray. Seconds later came the echo of cannon fire.

"Nine-pounder. Ease good shot. You?"

He meant could I shoot. I'd never shot a gun. Not even with Uncle Uncle. Mom wouldn't allow it. Once, she'd caught me shooting crabs in the creek with a neighbor's BB gun. Grounded me for two weeks. I shook my head.

"If you sail deez waters, you will learn to shoot and to shoot well."

Their next shot smashed into our mast, snapping the wooden spar, which fell across the transom, burying me among sail and ropes. The skiff turned and tipped further onto its side before rocking back and forth and coming to a stop. I scrambled from beneath the pile of splintered sticks, tangled ropes, and canvas.

"Keep the dog close." The old man put his hand on my shoulder. "He will lead you home to your papa, no? Only you must learn to speak as he does."

Water rushed in, filling the small skiff.

"Why're you telling me this?"

"You will be famous in deez waters, Señor Ricky. And save others. Only you must not let los bandidos find dis dog. Learn of how special dis dog is, and dey will kill you, of dis you can be certain."

I waited for the old man to surface.

He never did.

Alone except for the stupid smelly dog, I wondered at the old fisherman's strange words. How in the world could a smelly mutt I hardly knew lead me back home? Or speak to me for that matter? I studied the fractured rigging of our skiff, then the treacherous reef ahead, and finally the black ship that had by this time run up the skull and crossbones. Too far to swim and with no way to sail, I searched for some sort of weapon. I settled for the long, curved sail-rigging needle. If I couldn't flee, I'd fight.

It seemed like the smart move.

Which goes to show you that the dog wasn't the only stupid one in the boat.

CHAPTER 5

MY STUPID PLAN

The curved needle fit nicely in my palm. Using the extra sail thread, I bound the needle to my middle finger, leaving about two inches exposed beyond my fingernail. When I cupped my hand, it became a claw. It wasn't much of a weapon, but it was all I had and certainly better than a pair of bony fists.

If I thought I was going to fight off a ship of pirates with a sailing needle I was an idiot. Sometimes reading pirate books can make you do dumb stuff.

"Bring it on. We'll see what kind of pirates you are." Sometimes reading pirate books can also make you say dumb stuff to yourself.

I crawled forward, bent down, and looked under the small compartment that formed the front deck of the boat. The shelf across the bow was perhaps two feet deep and just wide enough for a man to kneel. Beneath the shelf the storage area offered better cover than the open cockpit of the skiff. I turned, sat, and scooted back. Without the old man's weight, the skiff took on less water. Still, six inches or more covered the floorboards. More rushed in.

By wedging my back into the narrow compartment, I could tuck my legs and almost fit under the shelf without any part of me sticking out. I bunched the fallen sail over the opening and my feet. Then I waited.

You may be wondering what I hoped to accomplish. To be honest, I wasn't sure. I didn't really have what you would call a great plan. I had the beginnings of a plan (hide), that's it.

Waves rocked the skiff, sending more water sloshing over my feet. With my free hand (not the one with the curved needle) I fingered the pendant and wondered why the old man would swear he'd sailed with Dad, who had clearly died in a fiery truck crash when I was younger. Mom had the news clipping articles to prove it. I shifted my position, giving my backside a break from the hard rib of planking that pressed against my hip. Legs stretched; a toe cramped.

Minutes passed. The crashing of waves on the reef became a dull roar.

More minutes passed.

A new sound: the slurping of waves, the murmur of voices. I scooted back.

I silently counted off seconds, trying to guess how close they were.

There came a grunt of effort; the skiff tipped. A board creaked.

Through the white shade of sail I saw a dark figure rise from the back of the boat. I held my breath. From the shape of the shadow, he seemed to be twice as wide as the old man and much taller. His silhouette bent forward, sifting through ropes and pulleys, throwing stuff over. The point of the needle clutched in my hand felt flimsy and small.

Some distance away … "Survivors?"

"Nay. Must've been blowed ter bits or jumped overboard. Bloody mess our guns made, too. But this mainsail, it'll make a fine shade on deck."

"Leave it be. We got sails enough aboard. Check fer a pouch or purse. Maybe there be some coins."

From the back of the skiff came grunting and thumping followed by growling and barking.

"What the devil be that?" the distant voice called.

"Dog, Squire."

"A dog?"

"Aye."

"Leave it be."

"But it'll make a fine stew, it will. Boys ha'n't had a good stew in—OOOW!" More grunting and growling, barking and bashing of wood. "Sorry mutt bit me."

"Told ye to leave it be."

"Here, boy. Come ter Two Pin Jim."

"Would you stop messing around? Drown the mutt and be quick about it. We don't have all day."

More cursing followed by snapping and yapping, then wild thrashing and water splashing. I hoped the old fisherman was wrong: that the dog was not my way back home even though the mutt was my only connection to Quiet Cove. So there was that. A deafening silence fell over the skiff. I waited, hoping that the big fellow at the back of the boat had left. But then the skiff tipped again and I knew he was still aboard.

Which meant the dog was dead.

"Is the dog dead?"

"Stupid mutt won't hold still. Can't get that knife ter his throat."

"Ah, for the love of the Crown. Hold him up. I'll shoot him myself."

"Aye, aye, sir."

Even now I can't explain why I reacted as I did. Sometimes I do dumb stuff. Like what I did next. I threw off the sail and rocketed forward, lunging toward the huge shadow.

The hollow barrel of a flintlock pistol pointed at my eyes stopped me in mid-lunge. Out of the corner of my eye I saw scruffy, mangy-looking men in a long, wide skiff staring at me. The sunbaked sailor with the pistol pointed at me wore a hat made of black banana peels. He had a jack-o'-lantern smile and three brown stumps for teeth.

With his free hand, the man with the flintlock pistol held the dog by its fur. "Your dog?"

"No."

"No?" He turned the pistol from me to the dog, all but pressing it in the mutt's ear. "Then ye won't mind if I kill it?"

The dog whimpered and wiggled, trying to break free.

"He's a special dog. Can talk to people."

"That so?" said a fancy-dressed man in the skiff. "What is this talking dog saying right now?"

"Don't know. I can't understand him. But you'll definitely want to take the dog and leave me."

"A talking dog would make a nice prize, Squire."

"Shut up, Jim." Turning his gaze from the man wearing the hat made of black banana peels, the fancy-dressed man in the skiff said to me, "How 'bout this idea. How 'bout we shoot the dog and take you. What say you to that?"

I shrugged. It seemed like the smart move.

It wasn't.

The fancy-dressed man in the skiff shot the dog.

CHAPTER 6

CAPTAIN LAFOOTE

And missed. Which is how both the dog and I ended up on a pirate ship.

"By thunder, if I find the scoundrel that brought that mutt aboard my ship I'll cut out his tongue and leave it flapping on the deck like a sail in irons."

"One word about the dog and I'll slice your throat. Understand?" It was the voice of the fancy-dressed man from the skiff.

Without moving too much, I nodded my head.

The blindfold came off. I blinked against the harsh glare of the sun. The fancy-dressed man made a slashing motion across his throat, letting me know in no uncertain terms that I was to keep quiet about whose idea it was to bring the dog along.

A giant man with black boots reaching almost to his knees stood over me. His face was nearly hidden by a long, tangled beard of greasy pewter hair. He wore a dark-red frock with large gold buttons; a black sash tied tight around his bulging waist kept an arsenal of knives and pistols secured to his person.

Clenching and unclenching his fists, he barked over his shoulder, "Turtle Bill!"

A small spry man hurried forward. Keys jingled on his belt. One of the lenses was missing from his metal-rimmed glasses and his glossy dark bangs, wet with sweat, hung over his high forehead. He had a long, narrow nose, pointed chin, and slender neck like an egret's. Every time he swallowed (which he did every few seconds), his Adam's apple bobbed.

"Aye, Cap'n."

"I want the men to make a full search of this ship. Somewhere on this vessel there's a dog and I mean to find him."

"T-t-to be sure, if, if, if t-t-there's a dog aboard he'll be found. But are you s-s-sure it's not a w-wharf rat? Two P-P-Pin Jim said last night he found one big as the Queen's crown feasting on a slab of pork."

"That I did," said the man with the banana peels on his head.

"You insipid mongrel. You think I can't bloody well tell the difference between rat droppings and *this*?" The captain lifted the heel of his boot. The sight and odor of dog poop smeared on his boot's sole nearly made me barf.

"Shall I sound q-q-quarters, sir?"

"For a scupper-dog? I should say not. If you can't find one flea-bitten pup then I'll have you and the rest of the crew lashed to the keel and raked across the reef, am I clear?"

"Aye, sir."

As Turtle Bill hurried away the captain wiped the heel of his boot on my bare shoulder. "Who hauled this lubber aboard?"

"Found him aboard the skiff," said Two Pin Jim. I noticed some of his black banana peels on his hat had begun to curl on the ends. "Squire ordered us to bring him back. Said he could be worth a guinea or two."

The captain bent down and looked me over. He raised his eyebrow. He only had the one, like The Captain. A single hedge of bushy, black bristles.

Cupping me under the chin, he tilted my head upwards. "Did he, now? Why, he's no wider'n a mizzenmast."

I realized the dark creases on the backs of his hands were not skin moles, as I'd first thought, but scars. The tops of his cheeks were burnished to the color of copper and his wiry beard hung like Spanish moss, covering the collar of his coat.

In a gravelly voice he said, "We're a ship of war, Barbeque, not an island freighter hauling mangos and livestock. You ship aboard the *Black Avenger* you best be prepared to stand before the mast."

His breath carried the foul odors of tobacco and tooth decay. I stared straight ahead, refusing to respond. Not because I was afraid, which I was, but because I was holding my breath.

"I'll not have this lubber stumbling about my ship like some drunken carriage driver. If we're to make Santa Maria by four bells I need the decks clear of riffraff. Run him through with the cutlass and feed him over. Sharks need to eat, same as a man."

The tip of a sword pressed against my back. Let me just say that at this point my admiration for the Pirates of the Caribbean took a hit.

"See here, Captain! You leave that boy be. He's mine."

The fancily dressed Squire came hurrying toward me, pushing aside the other sailors who tried to block his path.

"Yours, is he? And I suppose you'll be thinking the *Avenger* is yours, too."

"We have an arrangement."

The captain hesitated, and then slowly slid the sword back into its scabbard. "Very well. State your terms."

"I've paid my fare to be aboard this ship, same as the others, and our agreement is that any I bring aboard belong to me."

"Ah, spoken like a man of the law is them words. But there's only one law that matters out here and that's the law of the sea. I says the lad is not worth the two shillings it'll cost ye to bunk him aboard my ship. What say ye to that?"

"Two shillings? Why, you charged nothing for the bushmen except the standard fare for passage."

"Ah, the law of the sea is a fickle mistress, Squire. Her wages shift with the tide. Ye want the lad, ye'll cover his bunk and food. And I'll not have him loafing about. He'll remain below until we reach Santa Maria. Them be my terms, take it or leave it."

"Very well. Two shillings it is."

"Per day." An evil smile spread between the captain's whiskers.

"That's preposterous! You can't possibly expect me to—"

"See here, ye ingrate. It's lucky fer ye I don't toss the whole lot of yer cargo over the side. Ye want to get them ter market alive, ye'll be obliged to watch yer mouth and remember who's in command." The captain spun on his heel and looked up into the rigging. "Ye there. Skinny Bob. Take this limp lubber below and clap him in irons."

The Squire took a half step forward, as if to protest. "But you said—"

"I know what I said. Was my words, they were." The captain placed his hand on the handle of a long pistol tucked into a wide leather belt. "Below decks, says I, and that's where he'll stay. He can bunk with the Madman from Madagascar. That big brute has been itching ter get a new bunkmate."

This is a drawing of me being led to the brig to meet my new bunkmate.

CHAPTER 7

THE MADMAN FROM MADAGASCAR

At that very moment the Madman from Madagascar arrived on deck.

He was taller than me, taller than the captain, in fact. Also, he was a barrel-chested, bull-necked man with shoulders baked brown by the sun. Picture LeBron James only with less body fat. Long, sinewy forearms rippled as he reached down and grabbed the rope that bound my two wrists.

I began to think the old man had been right to jump from the sailing dory and swim away. I wished now I'd done the same.

"I smell shrimp," the Madman from Madagascar growled, grabbing me by the hair and yanking me onto my feet.

For a moment I thought he would let go and give me a chance to walk on my own, but then the Madman from Madagascar boxed me hard in the ear and sent me tumbling forward.

"Faster you walk the sooner the Madman gets him some loving."

While I lay there on the deck, hurting, humiliated, I thought how this would look on TV if this were the end-of-the-first-quarter recap.

ERNIE JOHNSON: Well, Charles, how do you think things are going so far for the underdog Bradshaw?

CHARLES: You got to believe in yourself. Take me for instance. I believe I'm the best-looking guy in the world. Certainly on this set. But this Bradshaw kid is out of his league and I believe he's going to get crushed. He's got to bring something stronger than what he's shown so far or else he's going to get killed.

ERNIE: So you think he's in trouble?

CHARLES: Ernie, it's called defense and that kid isn't playing any. I mean I wouldn't know anything about it personally, but I've heard about defense through the grapevine.

KENNY: Can I jump in?

CHARLES: I don't know, Kenny? Can you still jump? I've seen you shoot. Not bad. And you're quick on a fast break. But jump? Brother, you're past your prime. I've seen turtles get better elevation.

KENNY: I think we need to look at this kid's background. First, it's obvious he comes from a distressed background.

CHARLES: Let me stop you right there, Kenny. Alabama is distressed. Brothers in Kenya are distressed. This kid is Monica Lewinski with an hour special on HBO.

KENNY: Single mom, home alone on Christmas …

CHARLES: That's another one of those movies about a white kid that brothers don't watch.

KENNY: Apartment burns down, dog steals his pizza, he suffers some sort of medical episode, falls into a creek. Maybe drowns. Then he's rescued by a crazy old man who claimed the boy's father might be alive.

CHARLES: What's your point?

KENNY: He's carrying a lot of baggage.

CHARLES: Kenny, there's brothers all over America still carrying bags for white folks. It's called Amtrak.

That was the scene that played in my head: EJ, Charles, and Kenny recapping my pirate performance. Sometimes the things I see and hear in my head scare me.

That's when I did something dumb; I fought back.

I came up fast with both fists, catching the Madman from Madagascar just under the chin and snapping his head back. The blow drove him back with my right shoulder, shoving him into the captain. I took two wobbly steps toward the ship's rail. Sharks or not, I was going to jump over and take my chances in the sea. But before I reached the rail and jumped, the Madman clubbed me in the back of my neck with his fist. A powerful blow to my ribs turned me around; another landed square on my chin. Still trying to fight back, I took another half step.

Then my legs buckled and I went down to my knees.

"He's got some fight in him," said the captain. "More'n I'd have thought from the looks of him. Not too many men on this ship can take a punch like that. Ye still want to waste yer money on a lad like that?"

"Cargo like him should sell well. Might make a decent cabin boy some—"

"Caught'm, Cap'n! Dog was in the a-apple b-b-barrel."

A mob of men rushed toward us. Wiping blood from my lip, I lifted my head. Turtle Bill had the dog by the nape of its neck.

"Toss him."

"B-b-but the little fella likes me, sir. See how he's l-lickin' my hand?"

"And a licking ye'll get if ye don't toss that mutt right now!"

Turtle Bill sighed and raised his arm back to fling the dog over.

"Let the dog go."

The captain wheeled and stared at me. "What did ye say, boy?"

"The dog hasn't done anything wrong except be a dog. Give him to me. I'll make sure he stays out of the way."

The captain glowered, his single eyebrow twisting into a furrowed wooly worm.

"Giving orders to my crew, are ye now, Barbeque? Sticking yer nose in where it don't belong. Perhaps ye be thinkin' ye'd make a better cap'n than me?" Each time he spoke, a shower of saliva spackled my face.

"Best keep quiet," said the Squire. "Else things will go bad for you."

I could not disagree with the Squire's assessment of things, but I sort of believed the old fisherman. Not that I spoke dog. But the mutt was my only connection to home.

"It's my fault he's aboard. I should have never tried to save him in the first place. But I did and here we are. If you want to kill someone, kill me."

I don't know why I said that. Sometimes I say things without thinking first.

"Ye would trade yer life for a dog's?"

I nodded. Walking back what I'd said did not seem like a smart move.

The captain turned to the crew standing around him. "Hear that, ye scurvy swags? This pathetic excuse for a swab has got more pluck than any one of ye. Why, I'd like to know which of ye would trade their life for a dog. Well?" The men around dropped their gazes and looked down and around but not at the captain. "Figured as much." The captain eyed me. "'My life for the dog's,' says ye. 'Kill me instead of him.' We'll see if ye still feel that same way when the whip is against yer flesh. The Squire might own ya, but I still command this ship."

The captain glanced at the Madman. "Tie him to the mast and give him the lash. We'll see what kind of material he's made of."

"You'll do no such thing," said the Squire. "By rights the boy belongs to me. We have terms."

Before the Squire could take another step, the captain pulled a pistol and aimed it at his head. "By rights he be yers, that be true, but I am still the law in these here waters."

The Squire looked at me, at the dog, at the captain, at me, the dog, the captain, me, dog …

"What about the m-mutt, sir?"

"Toss him."

At that very moment from the crow's nest came the call, "SAIL HO!" (Fancy pirate term for: "*Hey, guys, you need to stop arguing about that dumb dog and come look. There's a ship out there and if we hurry we can catch it.*")

Which is exactly what the crew of the *Black Avenger* did next.

Right after Turtle Bill tossed the dog over the side.

CHAPTER 8

A PIRATE'S PRIZE

Men lined the quarterdeck (the part of the upper deck behind the mainmast), poop deck (the area behind the mizzenmast aft and atop the cabin roof), and forecastle (the upper deck forward of the front mast), awaiting their assignments. I knew all these boat parts from reading lots of sailing and pirate books.

Turtle Bill shouted commands, ordering men about. I remained by his side. High aloft standing on the spreaders a small band of men moved quickly into position.

I suppose he noticed me watching because he said, "Sharpshooters. D-don' even think about runnin' and trying to jump ship. With t-them in the rigging you wouldn' make it ter the railing before they'd cut you down. Best ter fight and die like a man."

"I wasn't thinking of trying to jump ship."

Jumping ship was absolutely what I was thinking.

"You weren't?"

"I was wondering why he didn't have his archers in the crow's nest."

"W-w-why would we d-do that?"

"So when we got close they could shoot burning arrows into their sails. You do have archers, don't you?"

He eyed the top half of the mast. "S-sure we's got 'em." Turtle Bill turned towards the man with the black banana peel hat. "Two Pin Jim, rustle us up some men with bows and arrows."

"Why?"

"Jest do it!"

"Aye, Bill."

"Good call," I said.

"Shut up." Right then the captain arrived to check on things. "All f-fitted out, Cap'n. W-w-where do you want him?"

"Bowsprit will do nicely." LaFoote pointed toward a short platform jutting off the bow. "He'll make a fine target up there."

I did not like the sound of that. Unfortunately for me, I had zero say in the matter. Lines and ropes ran from the forward mast to a compact deck hanging from the front of the boat.

"Watch fer coral and rocks. And don' be shy 'bout singing out if ye see the bottom rushing up to meet our keel." Then he rounded on Turtle Bill. "Order the men ter stations. Captain of that freighter will make a run for it once he learns of our intentions."

Turtle Bill sang out (literally, in a quivering falsetto voice), "To arms, men! To arms!" With a hard nudge in the back from Turtle Bill, I began to walk toward the front of the ship. "Best find a way to keep yer powder dry. Yeh'll be wantin' ter fire back if the crew of that merchant vessel decides to fight."

"I'm unarmed."

"In that case duck."

"Suppose I survive. The fighting, I mean. What's my share of the 'prize' as you call it?"

"Ya being a landsman, and just a lad at that, yer haul would be less than half a share."

"Is that a lot?"

"Depends on the prize. All we takes is handed over to the cap'n. Anyone caught with so much as a shillin' kept to himself loses his share. Or if yer found out like Thievin' Tom and caught more'n once stealin' from the brethren, then it's Davy Jones' Locker fer ya. The wounded, they get theirs first. A man loses an eye, leg, or arm, he gets six hundred pieces of eight. Fingers and toes fetch only one hundred. Got more of 'em to lose, don' ya know."

"How many men on board?" I asked.

"Ah, now yer gettin' ter the heart of the matter. See, the cap'n, he likes ter sail with a thin crew. Means more fer the men … an' him. So, on a ship of this size, carryin' twenty-four guns, that'd be seventy men or more. But only half of 'em need be experienced seamen. That's why he cut a deal with the Squire to keep ya. Even if yer killed and the cap'n loses the two guineas he paid fer ya, ya still present a strikin' figure up here. A youth like yerself with all yer limbs sends a signal ter the other ship that there's a captain aboard who attracts men with courage. Lightnin' does the work but it's the thunder that sends 'm runnin', don' ya know. That's the way of the pirate. Strike with fear and kill if ya must."

I eyed the ship off our bow. "What type of vessel is she?"

"I'd say from her shape and sails a small galleon. With that flag can't be anything other than Spanish."

We'd reached the bowsprit; he shoved me onto it.

"Now stand yer ground. And don' get any foolish notions in yer head. Ya wouldn' last five minutes in the water if ya was to jump. Not once the sharks get a whiff of yer blood."

Seconds later, alone and clinging to ropes and railings, I leaned forward for balance. With the heaving sea directly below me it was like trying to stand in a roller coaster car. One misstep and I would fall into the waves and be crushed beneath the hull. With each plunge into the sea, spray flew up and over me. Within seconds I was soaked. Behind me sails billowed and snapped.

But I had no idea what I was getting into. To be honest, if I hadn't been so confused as to how I got there, or afraid of what was to come, I might have enjoyed it more.

I'd been standing on the bowsprit for perhaps ten minutes watching the freighter when from amidships came a call from the captain. "Guns ready?"

I looked back to see Turtle Bill hanging from the rigging, surveying the men.

He answered the captain, "Double-shotted, as ordered, sir."

Lowering his spyglass LaFoote called, "Run up the colors! We'll see how the rabbit runs when the fox is at her heels."

I can't say it was with pride that I watched the men in the crow's nest unfurl the black flag, but a rush of excitement did sweep over me. I mean, it *was* a pirate ship and I *was* the bowsprit boy. How could I not be excited?

Instantly the ship was alive with cheers and howls spiced with bold curses and threats.

"Hey, ya sorry picaroon!" The call to me came from the rigging where Turtle Bill stood leaning out, one hand on the netting. "Yer supposed to be lookin' ahead!"

The helmsmen brought the wheel over; the ship surged forward, gaining speed. Waves careened off the hull, sending a geyser of spray into the air. Within minutes we had cut the other vessel's lead significantly. In the distance I could make out the freighter's crew hurrying into position.

"How's she rigged?" bellowed LaFoote. "For fight or to flee?"

"She's t-t-turnin' off, sir," yelled Turtle Bill. "And t-tryin' ter make for the lee of that island."

"Very well, we'll give the appearance of letting her slip away and then catch her on the backside of that island where she'll have less room to maneuver."

"Is that wise, sir? Ter let her out of sight?" Turtle Bill dropped onto the deck.

It had not occurred to me that anyone would dare question LaFoote's commands, but Turtle Bill spoke as more an advisor than crew. Within moments, the two men joined me near the front of the great ship.

"I wager that skipper will relax once he senses the danger has passed," said LaFoote, one huge boot resting on the platform. He stood with such ease, moving with the rhythm of the ship's lift and fall that he seemed almost to be dancing with the sea. "I mean to spare my ship and men, if possible. Even outnumbered and built for transport, that freighter will put up a hard fight. And given our destination and cargo, we'll need all the crew we can. Bill, have the helmsman take her to windward twenty degrees. We'll skirt the coast and catch them on the other side, unawares. You, boy, you keep a weather eye out. There'll be a frightful current running off the point of that island. I don't want to get swept onto those rocks when we make our turn. Them breakers will do us more harm than any guns that freighter may fire our way. Do I make myself clear?"

I nodded without looking back. No way I was going to try to turn and make eye contact.

"And a word to the wise, Barbeque. Ye best be careful talking to the crew. Mutinous lot, some of them be. Squire's nephew be the worst. Sniveling little mama's boy is always whispering ter other crew and trying ter stir 'em up."

That was the first I'd heard that the Squire had relatives aboard. But to honest, I was sort of glad.

41

LaFoote marched off, barking more orders and threatening to shoot any man who showed fear.

For the next few minutes, we raced toward the island. Giant plumes of spray exploded each time our bow plunged into the waves; the wind whistled as it blew across our sails. In all my years of watching the *Pride* from my apartment I'd never actually imagined I'd be standing on the bow of a pirate ship. I knew it was all part of the episode I was experiencing. Still, standing on the bowsprit with my hair flying back and the sting of salt on my lips and sea racing up to meet me ... I cut a stirring figure.

If only Becky Nance could see me now, I thought.

Gradually we began to turn and claw our way along, running parallel to the island's ragged coast. As we did, the profile of the freighter showed full in the golden rays of the sun. She was a remarkable sight, her cream-colored sails full of wind, the hull a vibrant green. In a few minutes the freighter was past the tip of the island and out of sight.

We were now close to shore, less than a mile away. There came the familiar scent of land, the sour odor of wet soil, and the sweetness of trees and plants. A cascading waterfall plunged into the sea, producing a mist that cloaked the banks of a steep valley. The sun's rays cast long shadows, painting the hills in shades of purple and pink. For a few minutes I wondered why the island looked so picturesque. Then it hit me. There were no houses or roads. No beachside hotels or condos. Just hills of green bathed in the shimmering moistness of an afternoon shower.

I suppose I admired the postcard scene too long, for I barely noticed that the crashing waves were growing louder. We were approaching the far end of the island where a long reef jutted out from shore. I guessed that the freighter was long gone. At least, I hoped so. I needed more time to plan my escape.

"Ready about! Hard alee!" LaFoote's voice boomed over the rattle of sails and rush of water.

The *Black Avenger* swung her bow, pivoting smartly as she cleared the edge of the reef. For the next few minutes she seemed to be sailing straight for the island. Then I saw it. What I'd thought was one island was actually two, separated by a narrow passage of less than a mile wide.

The reflection of the sun's rays bouncing off the water turned the sea copper. The *Black Avenger* surged forward, racing through the channel. On either side of us white surf broke over shallow reefs. Swells swept past, crashing on coral with thunderous regularity. Far ahead, past two islands, I saw a lighter shade of blue.

Beyond that, the open expanse of the sea and the freighter. She was still sailing south, sails trimmed but limp. The island now blocked her wind. The vessel wallowed along, struggling to gain speed. LaFoote had guessed right: the freighter was a sitting target.

"We're gaining on her, sir," yelled Turtle Bill.

I looked back. LaFoote raised a spyglass to his eye. "Ready the long guns. We'll strike a blow and see if she'll run up the white flag."

The words had no more left his mouth when something whistled past my head. It slammed into one of the lower spreaders, snapping it off. One of the crew, a man with a withered hand and red bandana, tumbled from the rigging and crashed onto the deck. The cannonball had clipped him just below the knee. He screamed in pain as blood spurted from the stub of the remaining half of his leg. From the direction of the freighter came a booming echo. Focusing my attention back where it belonged, I caught sight of a second puff of smoke, this one from the deck of a much larger vessel that was now sailing straight for us. Behind it, more ships: a whole fleet of them, in fact. All flying the Union Jack.

It was a trap.

The freighter had been bait.

And we were sailing straight towards what appeared to be the English Armada.

Chapter 9

The Hunter Becomes the Hunted

Another cannonball whistled over my head, passing through the lower sails before smashing into the foremast. With an agonizing groan, the tall beam splintered and thundered to the deck, crushing men, scattering others. LaFoote glowered at me. I offered a weak smile, shrugged.

Before us lay a golden sky, shimmering blue water, and a fleet of ships so thick I could scarcely see the freighter. Whereas moments before we'd been the hunter, now we were the hunted and, judging by the number of vessels sailing toward us, greatly outnumbered.

From the poop deck LaFoote shouted, "What do ye make of their sails, Turtle Bill?"

"Man-of-war, sir. Th-th-they're sheetin' in tight and m-m-mean business."

Puffs of smoke erupted from the lead vessel. Another shot slammed into mid-deck, ripping away planks. The wind carried away the screams of men blown to pieces.

"Shall we return fire, Cap'n?"

"I should bloody well say so."

Turtle Bill stood where he remained in the rigging, an expectant look on the man's face.

LaFoote glared at him. "Well? Are ye?"

"Waiting on you, sir."

"For …?"

"To give the word."

"What word?"

"So. You said you'd say 'so.'"

"Ye insipid idiot. Give'm a bang, man!"

"Aye, aye, Cap'n. Return fire, lads! And make it count."

In our pursuit of the merchant vessel, we'd sailed into the narrow channel and were trapped. Should we have tried to turn and flee, which seemed to me to be the smart move, we'd have very little room to maneuver. On one side a long reef ran along the edge of the channel. On the other, marking the tip of the smaller island, a rock face plummeted into the sea. Maneuver too close to shore either way, and the *Black Avenger* would be dashed to pieces.

Another ball struck the mast, toppling the mizzen sail. Its huge canvas imploded like a giant balloon and crashed onto the deck, taking with it some of the men who'd been walking atop the spreaders.

"Mighty fair shot, I would say," a muffled voice said close behind me. "How far away, you think? Two miles?"

Turning around, I saw that another sailor—my size, my age—had crept to the bow. He had a pistol tucked in his belt.

The weapon seemed large and out of place on someone so young.

"Less 'n that," I said.

The collapse of the foresail, smoke from our own guns, and a jumble of splintered wood lying about provided the boy and me with some measure of privacy.

"Then you better figure a way out of this mess."

"Why me?"

"Are you not the captain's eyes? I heard him tell you to watch out for danger. It would seem you have failed."

In case you're wondering, I did not have a warm and fuzzy feeling about the boy.

"He was talking about rocks and reefs. He's the one who sailed into an ambush, not me."

"I doubt the captain will see it the same way. Nor will the rest of the crew. Bowsprit boy is supposed to sound out the first sign of danger. Every sailor knows that."

"Look, why don't you go back to wherever it is you're supposed to be and let me do my job?"

"Making sure I stay alive *is* my job. And I dare say the rest of the crew would see things the same."

Before I could respond, a volley of musket fire swept across our bow, peppering the deck with hot lead.

"Give 'm another bang, boys!" Turtle Bill yelled. "Let 'm know we mean to stand by our colors."

From beneath me I heard and felt an explosion as our bow gunners returned fire. The deck heaved. Ahead on the approaching warship a pair of holes opened in the man-of-war's mainsail. A cheer went up among the crew of the *Black Avenger*.

"Well ..." said the boy. "I'm waiting."

"For?"

"You to come up with a plan for how to get out of this mess. And it better be a good one."

Turtle Bill shouted from aloft, "Ships still be comin', sir!"

Another round of cannon fire unleashed beneath me. Suddenly I thought of all the gunpowder that had to be on board.

Quickly I jogged toward the back of the ship, stepping over wounded men, slipping on blood, all while trying to avoid getting shot. I bounded up the steps of the poop deck, approaching the captain. "How much gunpowder do we have?"

"What in blue blazes does that have ter do with anything?"

"How much?"

"Enough ter keep up a fight and more."

"Have the men bring some of it on deck!"

"And have that man-of-war fire inter the kegs and blow us ter kingdom come? Are ye mad?"

"We'll lash several barrels together, come about, and drop them off our stern. They'll act as depth charges."

"Turtle Bill! What's this boy jabbering about?"

"Dunno, Cap'n."

"But don't you see? When that fleet of warships sails into those kegs of gunpowder our sharpshooters can fire on the barrels and blow them up. It might not be enough to sink them but it could buy us enough time to get away."

"Ah," said Turtle Bill. "Now I s-see what he means. Tried something similar, we did, off Santa Rosa after we'd captured that Dutch freighter."

"Right ya are," said LaFoote, stroking his wiry beard. "Our shooters must have fired three rounds of musket balls into those kegs and not one of them exploded. Almost lost my crew and ship on account of that blunder." Looking furious, he said to me, "Ye left yer position and ran all the way back here for that harebrained idea?"

"But it'll work, I know it will."

"Look, Barbeque. I gave ye one job. Keep a weather eye out for trouble. Now we got all the British navy breathing down our necks and a ship in shambles. Not ter mention the crew who's dead or wounded. Crew aboard my ship don't get promoted fer being stupid. They get lashes. Turtle Bill, get this sea urchin outer my sight."

"Aye, aye, sir." Aiming his pistol at me, Turtle Bill motioned to me that the meeting was over.

"Wait!" I said, pointing toward the longboats lashed to the railing. "How about we put some kegs in the ..." struggling to remember the pirate word for *longboat*, I blurted out, "gags!"

"He means gigs," said Turtle Bill.

"I know what he means, fool."

"We could lower the ..."

"Gig," Bill said, helping me.

"... And one of the crew could hide inside with the barrels. Then when the lead warship reaches the *gig*, the man in the *gig* could light the fuse and dive overboard."

"It'll never work," said LaFoote.

"Might," murmured Turtle Bill, "if we can get the gig close enough ter the frigate's hull. But we'll need a man who's willing ter die for the rest of us. Where aboard this ship are we going to find such a fool?"

"Right ye are there," said LaFoote. "Most of these men would kill their own mother to save their neck."

I was that man, of course. And in case you're wondering, I didn't volunteer because I was brave. I had a plan. And that plan was to paddle away as soon as the gig touched the water.

LaFoote looked down at his men bleeding and falling under the volley of gunfire from the warship. He seemed to catch the weight of the idea.

"Turtle Bill, pick a man who's hearty enough for the job. But don't tell him all that's involved. We'll spring that on 'im at the last minute."

Straightening my shoulders, I said, "Sir, since it was me who didn't see the warships in time how about if I ..."

"I'll man the gig, sir!" Looking over my shoulder I saw that it was the young man from before, the one who'd joined me on the bowsprit. He rushed forward carrying rope, fuses, and a small pouch of fire sticks.

"You?" asked LaFoote.

"I know you and the others think I am afraid and weak but I can do this, sir, I know I can. If you will give me a chance, I will prove my mettle." The boy thrust out his chest. I'm not making this up. He actually thrust out his chest. And for a boy his size, it was a substantially large and flabby chest. "Or die trying."

"See, Bill? Told ye there was something special about the Squire's nephew. Lad just needed the right opportunity ter prove he's stupid, is all. Very well, place the lad in a gig. As for this swab …" LaFoote said, glaring at me, "Lock him in the brig."

"For how long, sir?"

"'Til the Madman from Madagascar grows tired of loving on him."

CHAPTER 10

A KEG PARTY

"Wait, what? How come *he* gets to man the gig?"

"First off 'cause I says so!" When LaFoote said this he showered me with spit. "Second, I don't like ye. And third, 'cause I don't like him, neither."

"But it was my plan!"

"And a fine plan it was. Only, like I already said, I don't like ye. What's more, I don't trust ye. And yer out of uniform."

I looked down at my bare chest, bare feet, and ratty cutoff jeans. "Didn't know there was a uniform. The rest of the crew, they're wearing pretty much ..."

"Shut up! If that daft simpleton nephew of the squire wants to get himself blown up that's his business. Turtle Bill, get that gig ready. And see those casks are brought topside. Hurry, now. We've not a minute to lose."

"But are you sure one man is enough?" I asked. "With two of us we could make sure the gig is in place. One to paddle and one to …"

LaFoote rounded on me so fast I thought he was going to club me with his fist. "I've had all your flappin' tongue I can stand. The Squire's nephew is frail, foolish, and a prissy-pants."

He said this with the boy standing right next to me. For a half-second I sort of felt sorry for him, but the moment passed.

"Not worth two pence in a scrape, is he. Probably just get in the way and end up gettin' himself and others killed. Settin' off those charges, now, there's a mission he can handle."

"What about the boy's uncle?" asked the helmsman. "He's bound to catch word of what we're plannin'."

"*Ye* jest focus on turning this vessel around and getting us the devil out of this narrow passage."

"Aye, aye, sir."

Looking at Turtle Bill, LaFoote roared, "Can someone please explain why this muttonhead swab is still standing here? He should be in the brig by now with the Madman."

Turtle Bill shoved me toward the steps leading down to the main deck, my heart sinking. I'd almost reached the ladder leading down to the bowels of the ship when LaFoote bellowed, "Hold on there, Bill. Since it was the boy's idea and all …" My heart beat faster. "Make him bring them kegs of gunpowder topside. Then toss him in the brig."

Turtle Bill swung open the hatch and pointed below. "This way, swab."

"Ricky," I said. "My name is Ricky. Ricky Bradshaw."

"An' watch yer step. Found a pile of dog poo back 'n here earlier."

In all the excitement with the freighter and British warships (which were still pounding us with their cannons) I had forgotten all about the dog. Now I felt some guilt. And regret.

The dog was gone and with him went my only chance to get out of pirate land.

Backing down the ladder, I said, "What happened to your stutter?"

"Only does that 'round the Cap'n. Don't know why meself."

We reached the second level and paused on the ladder. Turtle Bill gestured toward a long, open room with its ceiling panels removed. "Boys be hot at work giving them Brits a bang, I'd say."

Portable walls had been stacked in a corner. Sails billowed overhead against blue sky. Men rushed about loading cannons, firing, pushing them back into place. A strong breeze blew, but the room remained blistering hot due to cannon fire.

On the next level we got off the ladder and passed through a small wooden door, walked down a narrow passageway, and back down another short ladder that dumped us into a much larger area. Inside were three long rows of what appeared to be huge caterpillar cocoons hanging from the ceiling.

"This would be yer bunk if ye weren't sleeping with the Madman."

The *bunk* was a threadbare hammock dangling from rough-hewn rafters. There was hardly enough space to squeeze into the swinging sack without slamming shoulders into the next man's rump.

"I can't imagine I'd get much sleep in one of those."

"Oh, ye would sleep jest fine. Come off a midnight watch when it's been rainin' and blowin' stink out and ye'll think this 'ere hammock's a feather bed, ya will."

"How come these men aren't on deck, like the captain ordered?

"Recoverin' from cuts and scrapes and such. Few of them got the trots on account of the grub. But never ye mind about that. A hardy lad like yerself, I'm sure ye got an iron gut."

Turtle Bill directed me through dark passageways where I found myself slamming shoulders and knees into doorposts and walls.

"Squire's nephew, Beckwith, he be a lubber like ye. And most likely jest as useless."

"Thanks."

"I only mention him as an example of how not ter be. Lad's been aboard for nearly three weeks and still don' know the difference between port and starboard."

"The Squire, what's the deal with him?" I said, trying to change the subject.

"Claims ta be a barrister. Swears he was a solicitor back in Wales. But he's nothin' more than a slave trader. Makes his livin' peddlin' those poor Africans he steals from the bush."

"And he brought his nephew along?"

"Maybe the lad is learnin' the trade. This voyage is the first I've seen of him. And the last, I hope. Acts like he's ter good for us. Everyone aboard the *Black Avenger* pulls his own weight, both crew and passengers. That's my say on the matter. But young Beckwith, he can hardly carry his own sweat. Always coming up with reasons why he can't stand his watch. Keeps ter himself, he does."

We came to a storage room filled with crates of vegetables and fruit. A large vat of water boiled over a low flame. I hadn't thought much about cooking aboard the ship until now. The idea that a fire burned hot in the middle of a vessel made of wood — and what seemed to be very old and dry wood at that — didn't comfort me. Nor did the aroma of the galley.

"I see the cook's been busy cleanin' out the cupboards. Most likely anticipatin' tomorrow's landfall."

"Landfall?"

"Santa Maria. The Squire, he needs to sell his cargo before the rest of 'em dies. Bushmen don' travel well over long distances." H bent over a kettle and spooned pea-green broth into a tin cup. He took a sip and, licking his lips, sighed. "Looks like we'll be havin' sea tortoises with a pinch of seaweed and albatross. Might be a tetch o' rat in it, too. Try some."

"No thanks." To be honest, I was trying not to barf into the large vat of grey, greasy, stinking, slop.

Another passageway and we came to a small, dark room. "Ah, here we are."

I should point out that keeping gunpowder close to the galley did not seem like a smart move. But it wasn't my ship, my plan, and I definitely wasn't going to volunteer to move the powder and armaments to someplace safer.

The kegs were relatively small. Each of us could carry one on each shoulder. Turtle Bill grabbed two and was gone before I could get the first up on my shoulder. For such a frail-looking man, he was quick and strong.

By the time we returned to the deck, the ship had reversed course and some of the crew had hoisted a gig over the railing. The boy named Beckwith received the four kegs and positioned them on the floorboard. The longboat hung precariously over wave tops while the crew tried to judge the distance between the swells. Slowly, the gig disappeared over the side. I ran to the rail and saw it skidding down the back of a wave, falling away. Beckwith released the lines and the small vessel turned, its bow pointing away from the *Avenger*. For a moment it looked as if the gig would capsize under the weight of the kegs and the rocking of the sea. But then Beckwith grabbed an oar and, guiding the bow up the face of the next swell, brought the vessel under control. Within seconds the gig slipped from sight, lost in the smoke of our cannon fire.

For a boy who could "hardly carry his own sweat," he seemed brave.

And knowledgeable about how to handle a gig.

And free of the pirate ship.

Which is what I wanted to be.

So right then I did something that is a perfect example of why boys my age should never be allowed to make decisions on their own without at least talking to their parents first.

I dove overboard.

CHAPTER II

JUMP SHIP

My great escape did not go exactly the way I planned it. The first problem was that I misjudged how far it was to the water. So while I had taken a big gulp of air before I dove over, I had used up most of it before I even hit the water.

Then I hit the water and the sudden impact knocked the breath out of me.

So that was a problem.

Over and over I sank as the ship's wake flushed me into a swirling washing-machine-like vortex that pulled me down. The murky green sea turned black; I lost all sense of direction. My throat burned, ears ached. At that point I was thinking that jumping ship was pretty dumb. Not really. At that point what I was actually thinking was: *I'M GOING TO DROWN!*

So I kicked.

At first it wasn't clear if I was kicking up or down, but I kept kicking. My thinking here was (A) I would eventually find the surface … or the bottom of the ocean, or (B) I'd be dead if I did nothing, so why not kick?

Turns out my plan, lame as it was, worked.

By the time I surfaced I'd already drifted a pretty good ways from the *Black Avenger*, which was fine with me since the whole idea was to escape. Except there was a new noise—and it was not the sort of noise that gave me a good feeling about being in the water. The noise was basically cannon fire and it was close. Very close. And getting closer.

The huge, dark shadow of the British man-of-war passed over me.

Whitecaps smashed into my face; smoke from cannon fire engulfed me. I pivoted and came so close to the great warship that I could have touched it. Right then an object struck me so hard I thought I'd been run over.

But it was not a great man-of-war warship. It was a boat oar.

"About time," Beckwith said. "Catch this." He dropped a powder keg on my head.

Well, not exactly on my head, because a wave washed over me at that moment, and I went under. When I surfaced Beckwith was saying, "I'll light the fuse, you hold the keg against the hull."

Before I could yell *ARE YOU CRAZY?* I heard the hissing of the fuse burning. I shoved the keg away from me and dove under.

A white-hot flash blew me backwards and down into the black swirling washing-machine-like vortex of the man-of-war's wake. Other than that my plan for jumping ship worked great.

CHAPTER 12

A PIRATE'S LIFE FOR ME

"Off ye go," said Turtle Bill. "Ye heard the cap'n. Clap ya in irons, says he."

"Can't I at least watch to see if my plan worked?" A muzzle flash let me know the warships were still firing at us, though they were much further behind than before.

"Keep moving, nothing ter see."

Beckwith gave me a look—one that suggested I should keep quiet. The truth was, my great plan had not worked as I'd hoped. We had disabled the man-of-war, sure. Now it lay sinking in the middle of the channel, preventing the ships behind it from pursuing us.

But here's the bad news: LaFoote had ordered the crew of the *Avenger* to reverse course a second time, fish us out of the water, and come about and sail away a third time. Which meant now I was headed to the brig to bunk with the Madman of Madagascar.

"Clap him in irons," said Turtle Bill.

"But we don' have any irons. Used the last set of irons on that feller that mutated and died from lashes."

"Skinny Bob means *mutinied*," Turtle Bill whispered to me. "Rope 'ill do nicely. Bind his wrists."

Skinny Bob, who was not so skinny, tied rope around the bindings on my wrists. His chest and shoulders glistened with sweat. I gathered from the way he whistled while he worked that he enjoyed the task of tying me up.

"Twinkle, Twinkle Little Star?" I said.

Pulling the rope tight Skinny Bob grunted, "Huh?"

"The song you're whistling. It's *Twinkle, Twinkle Little Star*, right?"

"Follow Me Up to the Gallows. Jest a little sump'en we sing when the rum's being rationed out."

"Bloody fool." A pudgy little man with a withered hand and a mop of gray beard hobbled over. "That's *The King's a Wee Little Locked*. Me mum sung it to me when I was a lad."

"And I say it's *Follow Me Up to the Gallows.*"

"King's a Wee Little Locked."

"Up to the Gallows."

"Little Locked."

"Gallows!"

"Gallows!"

"Little Locked ... " Skinny Bob, realizing his mistake, stopped and glowered at the little man. "Hey! You tricked me."

"Would ye two shut up?" said Turtle Bill. "To the brig with him!"

Skinny Bob shoved me towards the deck hatch I'd used earlier to reach the gunpowder room. Back down the ladder I went, only this time it was harder because my wrists were bound and ankles tied. As before we crossed the long room, only now scruffy seamen sat about eating the grey, greasy slop I'd seen boiling in the kettle. If you want to know what it smelled liked, imagine school cafeteria food that's been left sitting on trays for several days and boys and men sitting around belching and farting. That's what it smelled like.

"Stinks in here."

"You'll get used ter it."

Through a small wooden door, down a narrow passageway and up a short ladder we went, around a corner, and up a narrow dead-end hallway. Skinny Bob reached past me, inserted a skeleton key, opened the door, and shoved me in. He followed, pressing himself against me and my face into wooden walls with splinters. If you're thinking that two males in a closet leads to two males kissing in the closet then you have some idea of what I feared would happen next.

"Why are we in a closet?" I asked, hoping with all my heart I was wrong about Skinny Bob's intentions.

"Waiting."

From beneath my feet came creaking and clanking.

"Waiting for what?"

"Davy Jones. This be his locker."

"Does Davy Jones have a window in his locker we can open?"

"Lockers don' have windows. And windows be called ports."

The creaking, clanking stopped.

"Then why are we standing in a dark closet, talking."

"Wait fer it …"

I definitely did not like the sound of that.

Abruptly, the floor dropped away. I fell, not sure how far, and landed on top of Skinny Bob. Flies buzzed around my head. A stench, like the smell of a deer rotting on the side of a highway, made me wish I were back in the room with the grey, greasy slop where men farted and burped.

Trying not to open my mouth too wide, I asked, "What just happened?"

"We fell."

"Yes, but why did we fall?"

"Because we be Davy Jones' Locker and that be how Davy Jones' Locker works. See, the cap'n is big on swift justice and cheap entertainment, so durin' squalls we put them that's found guilty of crimes against the brethren in Davy Jones' locker. That ways they're not swingin' from the spreaders durin' a storm. Bad luck ter have a man swingin' from a spreader overnight. Careful where ya step. Not sure if them's Tom's bones or dried rat droppings we're stepping on."

I do not need to mention that the thought of stepping on rat poop or the rotting corpse of a dead pirate with bare feet left me queasy, so I'll skip that part.

From within the darkness and off to my left a voice whispered, "You there." I paused, looked in the direction of the voice but with it being pitch-black dark and all I couldn't see anything.

"Ye say something?" asked Skinny Bob.

"Coughed, is all."

"Wouldn't recommend ye do that ter much, Squid. Might frighten the bats? Now try 'n' keep up, else ye'll get lost. Wouldn't want that ter happen. Bilge rats big as that pup ye brought aboard be swimming around in this swill."

A hand reached out and grabbed me, which of course caused me to scream.

"Rat?" Skinny Bob asked.

But before I could answer, *no*, a hand jerked me sideways, pulling me through a door that swung shut behind me.

CHAPTER 13

SEA DOG

"You came aboard with a dog, right?" It was the boy Beckwith.

We stood in yet another passageway, only this one with more light and less dead pirate bones.

"What if I did?"

"I need to show you something. And we don't have much time."

The thought of spending the rest of my time aboard the pirate cruise ship bunking with the Madman from Madagascar did not leave me with the hope of pleasant vacation memories. On the other hand, I had been promised forty lashes if I did not stick close to Skinny Bob.

"Squid! Ye best not be hiding."

I glanced back at the small door that led to the bilge-water-sloshing, rat-filled, dead-pirate-remains basement of Davy Jones Locker. "Make it quick?"

Still holding my elbow, Beckwith pulled me until he stopped in front of a door. He rapped softly and a man's voice called, "It's unlocked."

"Ye best show yerself, Squid! Hiding from Skinny Bob earns ye twenty more lashes."

The boy shoved me in and closed the door behind us.

The room was tiny and hot, not much larger than my mom's bathroom at home. An unlit lantern hung from the ceiling. A round port window allowed a faint breeze to work its way into the room. Opposite a bunk bolted to the wall was a small desk cluttered with books and scrolls of parchments. A curtain divided the room in half.

"Doc has something he wishes to show you." Beckwith held back a curtain for me.

It hadn't occurred to me that there might be a doctor aboard but I was glad to hear of it. The gash in my hand still ached and had begun to ooze pus. The needle the old fisherman used had not been what you would call sterile and safe. And I had just swished my hand around in bilge water tainted by a rotting corpse.

"I'll wait out in the hall," Beckwith said. "If that big man comes by, I'll tell him you went the other way."

I stepped behind the curtain.

A tall, sallow fellow stood over a wooden table. He had a long, angular face, short white beard, and rimless eyeglasses. His balding head glistened with sweat. Beneath his black coat he wore a ruffled shirt.

Curled up in a chair, resting on a throw pillow, lay the dog.

"How did that mutt get in here?" I did not ask this in a friendly sort of way even though I was sort of glad to see the dog. "I thought he'd been tossed to the sharks."

"Apparently not. Doctor Flanagan," he said, offering me his hand. "Sailors ran past my cabin not more than a few hours ago, claiming there was a dog aboard ship. I waited until things quieted down in the hallway, then placed a piece of biscuit on the threshold. A dog will most always find a biscuit."

"And pizza," I said.

"This dog, he was with you in that sailing skiff?"

"Yes. The old fisherman thought he was mine. He's not."

"So then you do not know where he sailed from, where he is bound?"

"No idea. He's a stray, I think."

"Not a stray. A sea dog." The doctor pushed away fur and pointed to a tattoo etched into the dog's belly. "See those numbers?"

I did: and I'm ashamed to admit for the first time.

"This dog has been places, seen things. Sometimes a pirate will mark the location of where he's buried something of value by marking it on a trinket or perhaps a watch or medallion. Here, let me show you."

He walked over to a small desk and pulled out a scroll of parchment. With a pair of books and two candleholders anchoring the corners, he unrolled a chart.

"The numerals you see on the dog are degrees of longitude and latitude." Taking out a pair of dividers, he walked them from the edge of the map into the middle. There he wrote an "X" over a small island. "The coordinates on that dog's tattoo line up almost exactly with Isla de Ataúd."

"Isla de Ataúd?"

"Coffin Cay. A dreadful place. While I'm not one to believe in this sort of thing, men like LaFoote and his breed are convinced the island is haunted with the evil spirits of dead pirates swindled out of their share of treasure."

"The old fisherman who pulled me from the water said the dog could talk to people. But then he also claimed the dog could help me get back home."

"Perhaps he can. As I say, this one is special."

"And you think that dog is connected to a haunted island with buried treasure?"

"Not think. Know it. Every boy in Bristol has heard the tale of the dog that went to sea and returned with a collar of rubies and emeralds. The legend goes that a dog was found adrift on a raft floating in the River Thames. Some men from Southampton took him and had a ship outfitted for a long voyage. Three days out of port their ship sailed into a violent squall and sank. Only the dog survived. He washed up alive on the Isle of Wight. Before long another ship was outfitted, but it too ended in disaster."

"Sounds about right." So far the dog had brought me nothing but trouble.

"Boats and ships large and small have tried to sail with that dog and they all perished. Each time the dog would return … alone. Many a man has gone to the bottom on account of that dog. At any rate, the dog cannot stay here. He needs to go with you."

"Not gonna happen. I'm headed to the brig."

"But if the captain were to stumble upon these coordinates and find the treasure on Isla de Ataúd, then the balance of power could swing to the ill-bred Nation of Thieves. If it does, God help us."

I took a closer look at the tiny dot on the chart. "But if everyone else already knows about the island, then what's the big deal?"

"They know *of* the island's curse and its rumor of evil spirits, but no one has any idea of the treasure's actual location."

"So the island is haunted. Spirits of dead pirates are guarding a stash of jewels and gold. And the only one who knows how to find the stolen goods is this mangy mutt?"

"That is about the short of it."

"I read a lot. Too much, Mom says. And I know for a fact that most pirates didn't bury treasure. They'd spend what they stole on rum and wild living."

"Ah, to be sure, most did. But there's a bit of truth in every sea story."

"Whoever heard of a dog finding buried treasure? A buried bone, sure. Dogs like bones and dead stuff. But gold and silver?"

"Not just any gold, mind you, but Aztec. Enough to outfit a whole fleet of pirate ships, and wealth enough to buy the loyalty of every governor from Cartagena to Caracas. In any case, you have to make sure nothing happens to this dog."

I thought about what the old man had said. Of how he'd insisted that my father was alive, and that the dog could lead me to Dad and eventually back home. Reaching into my pocket I pulled out the medallion and handed it to him. "You ever seen anything like this?"

His eyes danced as he rubbed his thumb across the intricately embossed etching of the ship's wheel. Turning it over, he saw the name on the back. "Your father's?"

"So I've been told. Can you translate that inscription?"

He turned it over "'Esse Quam Verdi.' Latin for 'to be rather than to seem.'"

"Squid! Forty lashes be forty too few fer you."

Taking a final look at the napping mutt, who now stirred, I stepped from behind the curtain, opened the door a few inches, and peered out.

"Quick!" Taking me by my wrist, Beckwith all but flung me up the hallway. "I will stall him. Two rights, a left, down a ladder, then straight ahead. That will place you at the brig. Try not to get lost."

Which of course is exactly what I did.

CHAPTER 14

THE BRIG

I felt my way along in the belly of a ship that was dark and dank and stank. Rats torpedoed between my legs. Every few steps I cracked my skull against low wooden beams and tripped over thick hull supports. I was hopelessly turned around with no idea which way to go, but by following the stench of poop and pee I hoped to find the brig.

The ship bashed into another wave, sending a shudder down the length of its hull. Bilge water sloshed over my feet. Iron shackles had left my skin raw, allowing the salty brine to seep into open wounds. At last my nose led me to a compartment with two empty cells on either side of a submerged wooden walkway.

"Squid!"

The bad news was, Skinny Bob was approaching the brig.

The good news was, there was no sign of the Madman of Madagascar.

"Back here!"

Skinny Bob looked none too happy to find me standing outside the rusty cage that served as the ship's jail cell. "Ye ran off. Warned ye 'bout that."

"Didn't run," I explained. "Got turned around and lost." Which was partially true. I *had* gotten lost. And turned around. And done a few other things that I did not feel the need to mention.

Skinny Bob took the ring of keys hooked to his belt, which was a rope, and unlocked my cell. "In ye go."

I stepped in: waded in, actually. The stinking swill sloshed around my calves. From the looks of the two cells and water's depth, there would be no way to lie down and sleep. Not that I expected to get much sleep in such a vile place.

That was the bad news.

The good news was that Skinny Bob seemed to have forgotten all about the lashes I was to have received.

"The Madman of Madagascar 'ill be along shortly ter give ye them lashes."

He slammed the door shut, locked it, and left.

In case you're wondering, the first day on my Pirates of the Caribbean cruise was not what you would call a comfortable and pleasant ride.

CHAPTER 15

LASHES AND EYELASHES

The Madman from Madagascar arrived with a whip in his hand.

And a smile on his face.

And food in his teeth.

And an odor that reminded me of some of the passengers I'd met on DC's Metro late one night. Once Mom and I went to DC for a weekend vacation, but because my family doesn't have a lot of money, we stayed in a hotel that was only barely located in the United States. Which meant we had a long, late ride back after our day at the National Mall. Apparently the man sitting across from me that evening had also experienced a long, hot day enjoying the sights in our nation's capital, only he had not availed himself of the porta johns on the Mall like Mom and I had.

Anyway, the Madman from Madagascar reminded me of that individual, odor-wise.

The Madman tried the door, found it locked, and then reaching his beefy arm through the bars, cracked his whip. I jumped and quickly scurried to the back corner of my cage. At this point I was thinking, *As long as he's out there and I'm in here I'm safe.*

The Madman growled and tried again. His whip struck my bare shoulder. I screamed like a little girl.

"See here! Leave that boy alone!"

The Madman spun, as did I, and looked at the dark figure standing in the doorway. I think I mentioned how dark and dank it was in the belly of the ship so it was pretty hard to make out the person giving orders to the Madman. Let's just say it was not one of the crew. The person was too short, too thin, and wore an overcoat that, on a hot, stuffy ship like the *Black Avenger*, was unnecessary.

"You are relieved," the strange person said.

"Don' need ter go," said the Madman.

"I did not say *to* relieve. I said you *are* relieved. You may leave."

"But I ain' done." The Madman cracked his whip again.

Its tip sliced open my side just under a rib. Standing outside the cell and with limited range of motion, the Madman was extremely accurate with his lashes.

"This lad is the property of my uncle. Now leave."

Lowering his head like a scolded child, the Madman coiled his whip and skulked away, mumbling something about how he never "gets ter have any fun."

Once the Madman was out of range, the boy Beckwith said to me, "You are welcome."

Touching my side where blood oozed I asked, "By chance do you have the keys to this cell?"

"Oh yes. And the captain's stash of rum. And the flour the cook fails to use when he bakes scones. And all manner of accouterments necessary for raiding merchant vessels."

He removed the heavy coat and hung it on a peg beside the door. Shaking out his ponytail, the boy ran his fingers through his hair. It was at that moment I realized the boy Beckwith was not a boy at all. "You're a girl?"

"You stare as though you have never seen one before?"

I had, but not one that pretty. Well, Becky Nance, sure. Becky Nance was easily the prettiest girl on the planet. "But why are you a girl?" I admit this was not a brilliant question.

With the back of her hand she flipped the light-brown locks, allowing the curls to settle on the shoulders of her puffy, cream-colored shirt. "You think I would last five minutes with this gang of ruffians if they knew I was the governor's daughter?"

"What state?"

"Port Charles," she said.

Right. Of course. The United States isn't a country yet.

"My father swore to my mother that I would never set foot on his island. He dotes over me as if I'm still a child."

"How old are you, exactly?"

"I will be fifteen next month. If I were still in Bristol I would be announced to society already."

"Um," I said. I admit this was not a brilliant response, but with a girl that pretty standing in front of me that was the only word that came to mind.

"Anyway, the oath was my father's pledge to my mother. I did not necessarily agree with his decision."

"So does your dad know you're aboard a pirate ship?"

"He knows I am with my uncle, that is all." Studying me through the bars she said, "I have watched you, saw how you jumped ship to help me. You are not like the other men on this vessel."

"You mean because I have all my teeth, limbs, and eyes."

"There is that, I suppose. You have a confidence, a conviction that you are ... wiser than the others aboard this vessel. Even wiser than the captain. I could use an ally like that. I have a proposition for you. One that promises to pay handsomely if you deliver."

"Will this proposition of yours get me off this ship? Because off this ship is where I really need to be."

"We should make Santa Maria by four bells. The captain's intention is to remain at anchor in Santa Maria while my uncle ferries in his cargo to the slave market. I am to help my uncle. Then that vile rogue LaFoote plans to up anchor and sail for Port Charles. There he will free the men in the stockades, a good many of whom served aboard this ship. Of this I have heard him speak. Once he has a full crew, LaFoote plans to wreak havoc among the islands and cays near Port Charles. I mean to stop him."

"How?"

"By reaching Port Charles and warning my father."

"What does this have to do with me?"

"There is a small island that lies off the coast of Santa Maria. There a schooner awaits that will transport me to Port Charles. I could use your help. Even dressed as I am in men's clothing, I may be found out by rogues and scoundrels. I would prefer not to take that chance. You could help me reach the schooner."

I thought about this for like, a half-second, then said, "And die trying."

"Ah, there *is* that possibility," said Beckwith, batting her eyelashes at me. "Of course, I would be indebted to you." She tucked a strand of hair behind her ear.

I have to admit: at that moment I was actually considering jumping ship with her. Dumb, I know. I had no idea how me getting to Port Charles would help get me back home.

But at that moment with her still batting her eyelashes so hard she could have strained an eyelid muscle and smiling at me in a way that made me really wish the rusty brig-cell bars were not separating us, I said, "Sure. I mean, I dunno. Let me think about it."

"Squid!" It was not the voice of Skinny Bob.

"We'll talk more later," Beckwith said, slipping away before the tromping of heavy footsteps arrived.

Turtle Bill stormed into the brig.

Skinny Bob followed.

Behind him was the Madman from Madagascar. All had wet towels in their hands. Turtle Bill unlocked the cell. Skinny Bob—grinning with food between his teeth—stepped in. The Madman from Madagascar followed, bouncing his wet towel against his thigh the way a man might bounce a bull whip. A wry smile spread across Turtle Bill's face. "This'll be rich." The cell was basically the size of a trash dumpster and as I've explained it smelled about as bad. With the three men all pressed into the cell, Skinny Bob approached and yanking my face in his huge paw, he turned me toward him, and walloped me so hard on the chin that he knocked a tooth loose. "To help deaden the pain," he said. Then …

SNAP! Skinny Bob popped me so hard with his towel that I jumped clear out of the water. "Made me look bad in front of the cap'n and crew, squid."

"What he said, shrimp," growled the Madman from Madagascar. **SNAP!**

"'Cause this be the most fun I've had all day, swab." **SNAP!** Turtle Bill, snickering, snapped me a second time.

For a few seconds I clung to the bars on the far side of the cell and tried not to scream like a little girl. Basically the abuse was like boys in a high school locker room snapping towels at my backside. It hurt a lot but definitely not as much as it would have if they'd used real whips. But still, you know, it *hurt a lot*. Bullying is definitely not cool.

Closing my eyes, I thought about Beckwith's offer and pictured the two of us sailing away together to a nice, quiet cove ringed with palm trees with maybe a five-star tree house hut overlooking a secluded sandy beach. Below is a drawing of what I pictured in my head.

I did not really want the dog in the drawing but sometimes my mind adds stuff without my permission.

In addition to the dog, a few other thoughts entered the picture. You can't really see it real well, but behind the drawing of me lying on my side is a sketch of me holding up the medallion the old man gave me. The towel popping I was experiencing made me wonder if maybe there was a bigger purpose to me being thrust back into the age of pirates. Like maybe I was here for a purpose. Though at that particular moment my purpose seemed to be as target practice for three bullies.

The Squire wanted to sell humans as slaves, which we all know from studying U.S. History was a terrible idea.

Beckwith wanted to steal a schooner and sail to Port Charles to warn her father that LaFoote planned to free pirates from the stockade. Another terrible idea—the freeing of pirates, I mean. The two of us stealing a schooner didn't sound like a great idea, either.

The doctor had warned me to keep the dog close because the dog could lead LaFoote or some other pirate to a special treasure on some island that only the dog could find.

And the old fisherman had warned me that the dog could possibly lead me home and to my dead dad—which was just plain weird. So there was a lot going on in my head. I began to consider that maybe I was the main character in a really whacked-out pirate fantasy absence seizure episode that might hold consequences for my family and some other people's future.

But mostly this thought crowded out all others: *I NEED TO GET OFF THIS SHIP BEFORE SOMEONE GETS KILLED!*

Which, as it turned out, is what happened next.

CHAPTER 16

WHEN PUSH COMES TO SHOVE, KILL THE MAN

"L and ho!" The cry from on deck ceased the snapping and popping of towels on my rump. "Land ho!" is a fancy pirate term for: "Hey, guys, look. There's land out there and if we hurry we can hit it.") Turtle Bill and Skinny Bob rushed from the brig. Unfortunately for me, the Madman remained in my cell, only now instead of popping me with a wet towel, he licked my cheek with his sandpaper tongue.

"Land ho!" came the cry again. "All hands on deck."

"That means you," I said to the Madman from Madagascar.

The Madman paused from slobbering on my neck, a confused look on his face. "It does?"

"All means everyone. You *are* one, are you not?"

The Madman blushed, a confused look on his face. "How did you know?"

"I, ah …" Carefully, I extracted myself from his embrace. "Lucky guess, is all. You better hurry before the captain finds out you are derelicting your duty."

"Doing what to my doodie?"

"GO!"

To my surprise the Madman left. Here's what happened next.

First I did nothing. I needed to make sure the Madman was really was gone. Next I scurried up the ladder. My plan was this: jump ship. Having jumped ship once—and survived— I figured I was an expert over-the-side-of-a-pirate-ship diver. All I had to do was get to the main deck without being seen by Turtle Bill or the captain.

Two levels up I saw men backing down the ladder coming towards me, so I swung off and bolted through the long room where the cannons were being moved out of the way. They carried partition wall panels and were placing them back in position. None of the pirates paid any attention to me; my plan seemed bullet proof. I'll skip over a bunch of boring stuff about how I snuck down another passageway—the great ship had lots of ladders and narrow halls—and get to the big problem that caused my plan not to look so bulletproof.

"Hey, swab! W-w-why are you out of your c-cage?" Turtle Bill started yelling and running after me, only now he had his flintlock pistol drawn. "Troy," Turtle Bill shouted. "Get back here."

I noticed a ladder out of the corner of my eye, lunged for it, and missed.

POW!

Had I not been falling feet first down the ladder's shaft the musket ball would have probably nailed me in the back. Fortunately I landed on a pile of sweaty, smelly, and bloody pirate laundry. Which meant I'd falling into the ship's clothes chute. Rolling onto my knees, I bounded up and ran down yet another hallway, a short flight of steps, and found myself lost in a poorly lit area near the back of the ship. Fumbling my way along the hall, I felt for a doorknob to a cabin or closet, any place I could hide.

"He has ter be close!" Turtle Bill shouted.

"Squid!"

"Shrimp!"

Apparently Turtle Bill had brought a posse.

"One of ya stand here at this ladder in case he tries to sneak back this way."

I jiggled a door latch, found it locked, and moved on. I tried across the hall. Also locked. Behind me I heard the pounding of footsteps approaching. Pressing myself into a small alcove, I stepped back just as a pair of feet appeared at the end of the hallway.

"Put two men at every doorway," roared LaFoote. "I'll not have that muttonhead running about my ship."

Oh, great, I thought. The captain has joined the posse. I'm a dead man. My fingers fumbled with a keyhole. *If only I had something I could use to pick the lock. Belt buckle? Shoe laces? Paper clip? Who do I think I am, James Bond?*

"Aye, aye, s-sir. We'll f-f-find the lad."

I considered the medallion in my pocket, but decided its ship spokes were not nearly long enough.

"Show yourself and I'll let ye live, Barbeque. Not that ye'll be wanting to. Not after Skinny Bob and the boys finish with ye."

My hand found the curved needle the old fisherman had used to stitch me up. Its tip fit nicely in the hole. I wiggled the needle, heard a faint click, and the door creaked open.

"Heard something, s-sir."

"Well don' tell me about it, man, find the lad!"

I slipped in and quietly shut the door.

Heavy-looking trunks with leather straps and rusty locks pressed against my legs. Peering over the sea chests, I saw ceramic containers of varying shapes and sizes carefully arranged in one corner. Across the room, bolts of cloth lay stacked to the ceiling. Purple silk, coffee-colored cashmere, and tartan wool. Exotic fabrics made from faraway lands. The storage trunks rose like steps toward a wide window across the back of the room. A wisp of breeze caused a wine-dark drape to flutter.

A way out, I thought.

The rattling of the door latch caused me to stumble back and bump into a trunk that crashed into an urn, knocking its lid onto the floor.

"Found the rat!" LaFoote shouted.

I shoved the trunk against the wooden door and quickly dragged another in place behind it. There was no point in trying to pretend I wasn't hiding exactly where everyone knew I was hiding. But by wedging the second chest as I did, it formed a brace against the first. Which meant the pirates on the other side would have to bust down the door to get in. Which they could easily do if they put their shoulders into it.

POW! A musket ball ripped a hole in the door, leaving a perfectly round oval.

An eye appeared. "See ye, Barbeque. No way out."

The eye vanished. Before I could move, another shot ripped a second hole in the door's planking, hot lead narrowly missing me. LaFoote was very good with blind shots.

"Sir, yer n-needed on deck. T-t-there seems ter be some dispute 'bout the gigs and the Squire's cargo."

"Blast it all, Turtle Bill! Yer job was ter whip the swab till he bled ter death. And now here he is hiding like a bilge rat."

"Me and Skinny Bob 'ill guard the door till ye get back. Boy has no place ter go."

"The devil ye will. Send a runner ter see what the problem is. I need ye here." The latch jiggled, but the door didn't budge. "And tell them ter fetch the Madman. If anyone can bust down that door, it be him."

That wasn't exactly the news I wanted to hear. The Madman from Madagascar could have moved the defensive line of the New England Patriots all by himself.

Scampering up the pile of trunks, I climbed my way toward the window. Pulling back the curtain I looked onto the wide blue bay filled with ships and boats of all sizes. Below us, dockhands scurried along the wharf, unloading cargo onto wooden carts. Farther down the street, stately men in white straw hats exited carriages. Not far from the edge of a seawall, tents made from sails were strung between palm trees, providing shade for the men lounging about on the beach. I might have appreciated the view more if I had not been trapped in a storage room like a bilge rat about to be shot.

The trunk next to me had rotted through, spilling out necklaces, bracelets, and rings. Now I saw why LaFoote didn't want a guard to stand watch, and why he so badly wanted me out of the room. Apparently I was in the pirate ship's treasure room.

There came another loud grunt: the doorframe splintered.

I flipped the window lock and pushed it open. For a split-second I thought about jumping, then I remembered that I'd almost drowned the last time I'd tried that move. Quickly I tied the sleeve of a velvet dress to a rafter above my head and hung the rest of the gown out the window. It wasn't nearly long enough, but it would have to do.

Shoving trunks aside, I wedged myself between stacks of luggage and ducked down, turning sideways so I had a clear view of the door. I pulled one corner of a chest over my head so that I was partially concealed. If someone looked directly at the trunks they would only see a narrow, dark slit between the two stacks. *Keep quiet and don't move*, I thought. *They'll think you jumped out the window.* Look, I'm not saying it was a great plan, or even a good idea. To be honest this was about the only way I could have made the situation worse—which, of course, made perfect sense in my panic-filled brain.

There was a loud crashing sound; men barged into the room.

"Find him!" LaFoote stood so close I breathed in his stench. "NOW!"

Turtle Bill, Skinny Bob, and the Madman went about lifting lids to urns and ceramic pots ... opened small jewelry boxes, and turned pillowcases filled with jewels inside out.

"In the trunks, you three muttonheads! He ain't in no pillowcase."

"Sir, the window."

"Fool thinks I'd fall for that pretend-ter-crawl-out-the-window trick, does he. Crawl up there and check, Bob."

The stack shifted. My heart sank. Once Turtle Bill was on top looking down, he'd clearly see me. *Dumb plan. Dumb, dumb, dumb.*

Another voice called from the hallway. "Sir, it's the Squire! He asked if we might provide gigs for his cargo and if so how many?"

"Gigs? Fer them stinking bushmen? They can jump and swim fer all I care."

"Squire said you might say that, sir, so he wanted me to remind you that most of his cargo cannot swim."

"Oh fer the love of Lucinda. Tell him I'll be right there." Wheeling, LaFoote grabbed Turtle Bill by the ankle and yanked him off the pile, causing a storage trunk to conk me on the head. "Find that boy! I'll be back."

"Skinny Bob, you take that side of the room," said Turtle Bill. "I'll take the other."

"What about me?" asked the Madman.

"You move the trunks when we say so."

Turtle Bill had barely gotten the words out of his mouth when the door banged open.

"Hold on a bloody minute," roared LaFoote. "I see what's going on, now. The three of ye be planning ter take inventory, ye are. Perhaps keep some of what ye find fer yer own, are ye?"

"We were?" asked Skinny Bob. From his tone it was clear this thought had never occurred to him.

"I'll stay and look fer the lad. The three of you deal with the Squire."

"Aye, aye, sir."

The posse of pirates tromped away. Silence fell over the room.

LaFoote shuffled about, moving trunks and cussing each time a ceramic urn or pot crashed to the floor and broke. I held my breath, afraid to breathe.

"I know yer here, Barbeque. Only a fool would jump from that window. Problem is, I don't want to be opening all these trunks and crates 'cause some of this stuff wasn't exactly cataloged when it was brought aboard. If the crew were to find out that I was keeping some extra for myself then I'd have a bloody mess on my hands." A trunk lid creaked open and slammed shut. "So jest come on out and save both of us some trouble. Ye'll be shot, of course. But that's preferable to getting the lash from Skinny Bob and then getting shot."

I suddenly felt a strong urge to pee my pants.

Right then another voice interrupted the scraping and slamming of trunks being opened and shoved. "See here, Captain. What's this business I hear about you not supplying me with gigs for my cargo?"

"Business be business."

"What the devil is that supposed to mean?"

"No one knows. Only something some people say. And yer not supposed ter be in here."

"The gigs, man, I need them to ferry my cargo ashore."

"How ye get yer cargo ashore be yer problem, not mine."

"But the terms were plainly agreed upon before we set sail," said the Squire. "My cargo was to be delivered to the docks at Santa Maria. Now I'm to understand that we are to drop anchor only long enough for me, my nephew, and my cargo to swim ashore?"

"Each man kin have a deck plank, if need be. Can use that as a float."

"They will have gigs and help getting to market or mark my word, every sailor aboard this vessel will know you have dealt dishonestly with the distribution of captured goods."

"See here! I'll not be spoken to like that. As long as I am paying your fare and those of the crew ye'll address me with the respect I'm due."

LaFoote pulled two pistols from his belt and aimed them at the Squire. "I'll speak to ye any way I please."

The two men stood out of my range of sight, but it was clear from their tone that neither was focused on the stack of trunks. Which meant if I were going to escape, I needed to make my move. Quietly I placed one foot on the edge of a trunk and stepped, climbing towards the window.

You probably already figured this out: I couldn't have cared less if the Squire's so-called cargo reached shore. All I cared about was getting off the pirate ship and, if possible, back home to Quiet Cove. Which, I felt sure, would happen as soon as my absence seizure episode ended. Problem was my absence seizure episode was taking a long time to end.

Which made me wonder if—and here I had a sickening thought I definitely did not wish to dwell on—I had drowned in the creek. In which case I was dead and might never awake from this nightmare.

This is a drawing of what I saw.

"I'll wager that every man on this ship would rather be flogged than utter a cross word to me. But not ye. Oh no. For a lubber with no regard for the laws of the sea ye speak boldly, ye do."

"The only law I know is the law of justice and the Queen," the Squire shot back. "And you? You've set yourself to be king, queen, and judge. Your men might cotton to this sort of reckless behavior, but your brash talk does not scare me."

Now that I'd stepped onto the trunk I could plainly see the two men.

LaFoote grabbed the Squire by the lapels of his coat and jerked the man close. "Provide gigs, says ye. Provisions and water fer yer cargo, says ye. Not more than an hour ago ye leveled a pistol at me, thinking ye could threaten me like some beggar in Bristol. Well, sir, here be how I deal with any man who crosses swords with me."

Shoving the squire backwards, LaFoote quickly drew his cutlass and before the squire could protect himself, thrust it into the poor man's chest. Its blade sliced flesh and organs and didn't stop until it hit bone. The squire groaned and wilted, falling to his knees in slow motion. His eyes settled on the hilt of the cutlass, a look of shock and confusion on his face.

Lifting his eyes to meet LaFoote's the Squire said in a gargling voice, "You'll rot in hell for this."

"As will ye," replied LaFoote, and pressing his boot against the squire's shoulder, he pushed the body away and withdrew the cutlass.

Without waiting to see what the murderous captain would do next, I scrambled up the stack of trunks, threw back the curtain, and leaned out.

Behind me came the *CRACK-POW!* of his flintlock pistol firing. LaFoote's aim was almost perfect.

I tumbled out headfirst.

CHAPTER 17

RELAXING ON A CARIBBEAN BEACH

Beckwith's hand rested against the side of my arm. Surf boomed. A gull glided overhead, laughing. The gull was the only one laughing.

"He was my mother's oldest brother." She leaned her head against my shoulder. "I never felt at ease in his presence. He always looked at me in a strange way. Not like a relative should. That is why I asked the doctor if I could stay in his cabin to sleep and change. When the others left to go on deck to bathe, I could see my uncle watching me."

"Did he ever ... you know?"

"Heavens, no. The doctor, once he knew of my concerns, made sure there was always someone around when I was with my uncle."

"So you're not mad that he's dead?"

"Mad, no. Sad. He was, as I said, Mother's brother. But I am glad to be away from him."

"Why'd you agree to come with him on this trip? I mean, if he gave you the creeps like you say."

"I saw it as my chance to escape the dreary life of London. Most of the girls my age are in boarding school. I was set to enroll next month. Have you ever been to London? Horrid and dank it is. And dreadfully cold. I have seen what becomes of young ladies who attend those schools."

"What does become of them?" I asked.

"Now you are mocking me."

"Seriously, I'm not. This is all new to me. If you'd stayed what would've happened?"

"I would have learned to curtsey and bow and serve tea in silence while the men discussed important matters like the Crown and Her Majesty's latest edicts. I have always thought it odd that men would willingly obey the law of a queen but treat their wives and daughters like house servants. What about you?"

"Me?"

"Have you ever attended school?"

"Oh yeah. Sometimes that seems like all I've ever done. Except during summers and like now when I'm off for holiday break."

"Is that how you came to be on the *Black Avenger*? Are you on holiday?"

"To be honest I'm not sure how I ended up here." You probably already figured that I could not explain to her how I was having an absence seizure and while I was sitting right next to her on the sand—in my mind, anyway—I wasn't. Not really. "I live a long way from here, in America. And it was snowing when I left."

90

"You mean the New World. I have heard of it. My father writes about those who fled the Crown. He says they are nothing more than commoners who are too poor and stupid to know how good they had it in England."

"We're not colonies anymore. We're independent states."

"I doubt that. I am sure if the colonies had gained their independence from Great Britain I would have heard of it."

Like I say, me trying to explain that I was speaking of something that wouldn't occur for more than a century to come would only confuse her more. And probably lead to questions I couldn't answer. Better to keep quiet. That seemed like the smart move.

"What happens now that your uncle's dead?"

"Happens?"

"To the slaves."

"I'm not sure. The captain may try to force them to fight with him. Or he may just throw them overboard, as you heard him threaten to do. You are certain of what you saw?"

I explained again about how I'd snuck into the treasure room and hid, only to be found by LaFoote and almost killed. "If you had not slipped away yourself and seen my jump, I might be dead."

"So you might say we saved each other."

"Only now we're on this beach on Santa Maria without any way to find that schooner you mentioned."

She remained quiet. The *Black Avenger* appeared unusually dark and foreboding as it tacked its way out of the harbor. The good news was, I was alive. Bad news was, I seemed to be getting farther and farther away from Quiet Cove and Mom.

"I guess you are the only friend I have left," she said. "I mean, other than the doctor."

"Once we reach that schooner everything will be fine."

I had no idea if it would or would not, but it seemed like the right thing to say.

"Now you are simply trying to make me feel better."

"Did it work?"

"A little." She stood, brushing dirt from the back of her pants. "Better go get your dog."

Barnacle had cornered a lizard. A really big lizard. One of those sumo-wrestler-huge Komodo lizards. The two combatants eyed each other, hissing and making threatening animal sounds.

"My father has written to me about those monsters. They can grow to six feet long and have fangs three inches or longer. Their bite is fatal."

I whistled for Barnacle. Of course he ignored me. "I have to ask: why'd you bring the dog?"

"The doctor insisted. When I told him my plan to slip overboard and swim ashore he made me promise to take the dog. He said you would approve. It was easy enough and no trouble at all."

I whistled again. "Hey, you dumb dog, leave that lizard alone. Get up here!"

Beckwith moved her hand from my arm to my chin, brushing it with the back of her fingers. "You have whiskers."

I'm sure I blushed. My face felt like a red-hot apartment building on fire. "Forgot to bring my razor."

"I like it." Eyeing a small inlet emptying into the channel she said, "I bet if we will follow that creek as far as we can we will find high ground that will allow us to survey the island. Perhaps from there we can spy the schooner my father promised." She extended her hand and helped me onto my feet.

I whistled. Stupid dog continued to stalk the sumo-wrestler-huge Komodo lizard. "Guess we better go get that dumb dog before he gets himself killed."

Not arm in arm but almost, we walked down the beach toward the stupid dog. "If we are going to work together you may as well know my real name," she said.

"I'm Ricky. Ricky Bradshaw."
"Rebecca Evaline Vance."

Chapter 18

Santa Maria

We followed the meandering creek as it cut across the valley, pushing out into the jungle. Black soil oozed between my toes. Thick roots lay atop the ground like serpents, while overhead small birds darted in and out of the branches, their yellow feathers bright against the forest canopy. The dog stayed close on my heels, ears erect, its nose sniffing the ground. I spent the next few minutes pretending it was no big deal to be in the company of a young woman named *Rebecca Evaline Vance* who looked and acted almost exactly like Becky Nance. Same color hair, same length. Even her piercing green eyes and the casual way of tossing her head back when she appeared nervous was exactly like Becky's.

Then there was Captain LaFoote. Until that moment I had not thought much about how his rough and tough, drill sergeant personality was almost exactly like that of my teacher,

95

The Captain. And Turtle Bill had the stuttering speech of my shop teacher, Bill Pollard.

I think I mentioned how before, I had never, ever, been able to know I was having an absence seizure episode while I was having an absence seizure episode, but now I knew I was having an absence seizure episode. Only this time it was different. I could still feel pain on my backside from where I'd been popped with wet towels. In dreams you almost never feel physical pain. At least I don't. But my jaw still hurt from where I got walloped by Skinny Bob and the gash in my hand throbbed. It was like I was living my own version of *The Wizard of Oz*.

You know the story of *The Wizard of Oz*. The movie has only been around for like a gazillion years. They even made a Broadway play sequel sort of story called *Wicked*, which was even more popular. Mom loves *Wicked*. Has the soundtrack on her playlist. In *The Wizard of Oz* a nasty neighbor tries to have Dorothy's dog put down because it keeps getting into the neighbor's garden.

In my case I did not *own* a dog, did not *want* a dog, but I ended up *with* a dog.

Dorothy takes her dog Toto and runs away. I tried to save Barnacle and ended up flushed away.

A cyclone appears and carries Dorothy (on a bed) to a magical land. I fall into a cold creek, sink—maybe even drown— and a raft carries me to pirate land.

But all Dorothy wants to do is go home, so she begins traveling to the Emerald City, where a great wizard lives. On her way she meets a Scarecrow who needs a brain, a Tin Man who wants a heart, and a Cowardly Lion who desperately needs courage. So far I'd met a mean captain who reminded me of a mean teacher, a stuttering captain's mate who reminded me of my shop teacher, and a pretty boy who turned out to be a pretty girl.

Clearly Dorothy is a nice, normal girl. I mean sure, she's a little snippy at times, but she's protective of her dog, even if she does feel something missing in her life. Basically Dorothy is like a lot of kids in high school: she doesn't fit in, doesn't belong.

So anyway, while we walked I thought about how I was starring in my very own *Wizard of Oz* movie, only it was a pirate story set in the Caribbean, not a farm story set in Kansas. Like Dorothy, I desperately wanted to get back home to Mom and Christmas and my dreary, dull life at Quiet Cove High.

Rebecca clambered up some rocks. The sun had dropped behind the hills to the west and though neither of us had mentioned it, I'm sure we were both thinking that walking through a tropical jungle at night was a bad idea. Because I didn't want to spend too much time thinking about how Dorothy almost *did not* make it back home, I said, "What happens if you miss your ship?"

"I won't. The captain will wait for me."

"And if he doesn't?"

"He will."

That was it. That was the extent of the conversation. So I went back to thinking about how the Wicked Witch of the West almost killed Dorothy and her friends. Except in my case the mean character in my story was Captain LaFoote. And if he caught me he'd definitely kill me, since I knew he had hoarded extra treasure for himself in the treasure room and murdered the Squire.

After almost an hour of walking without talking we reached the summit of a high ridge that divided the island. Howler monkeys hooted in the trees above us. Before us lay a carpet of green hills, a deepening blue sky, and the sea with the sun's rays reflecting off waves. In the distance, beyond treetops, thatched roofs marked the edge of a small village.

Rebecca's gaze remained fixed on the distant cove barely visible above treetops. I, on the other hand, took a few steps down the steep embankment, trying not to fall.

"Now you have me thinking," she said.

"About?"

"The schooner sailing without me."

Great. Now I had transferred my fears to her. "It won't," I said, trying to sound upbeat. "See? We're almost to the other side of the island."

We were not almost to the other side of the island.

"But what if it has, what then?"

"Come on. We better keep going." Clutching branches for support, I continued backing down the slope, not catching up at all. Barnacle seemed to have golf spikes embedded in his paws. He darted from one slick smear of mud to the next, all the while sniffing the underbrush for whatever it is dogs sniff for.

"I have no money. And my papers of transport are back aboard the *Avenger*."

"We'll get you some new travel transport papers."

I had no idea where we would get travel transport papers. Mostly I was saying stuff in hopes that she would follow me down the slope. With the sun down below the hills the jungle was definitely darker than before.

A limb snapped.

Howler monkeys stopped howling.

I paused from backing down the steep, slippery slope and whispered, "Hush."

"Do not hush me."

With a finger over my lips I gestured for her to stop talking.

She folded her arms, glaring at me. Wind rustled the branches. Insects buzzed. A bird squawked.

"You're not familiar with the tropics," she said, unnecessarily loud. "There are always things in the jungle making noises."

"I know that," I whispered back too loudly. "But I think I heard …"

Before I could finish, a small dark blur shot past me, snapping off branches and crashing through the underbrush. The small boy, clearly lacking—pants-wise—in the wardrobe department, slowed only long enough to snatch Barnacle up by the fur of his neck. Then the pair continued skating down the hill, into the thick underbrush, and out of sight.

"… footsteps."

"Well … are you going to go after him?"

"The boy?"

"The dog!"

At that moment chasing an almost naked boy through a jungle was low on my list of fun things to do while lost in the Caribbean. Hiding behind rocks in case the boy was not alone, *now that* seemed like a good plan.

Rebecca shoved me before I could respond.

I went tumbling after the boy and dog, sliding and falling, tripping over roots and slamming off trees. The boy bolted through the tall brush like a gazelle. (Not that I'm all that familiar with gazelles, but I have seen lions chasing gazelles on YouTube videos and they look fast. So do lions.) I lumbered behind, cutting my feet on rocks and briars. Crossing a small gully, I scrambled up the other bank and followed Barnacle's yelping and snarling.

Smashing through a thicket of sharp fronds, I came to a narrow stream that fed into a wide, marshy swamp.

On the far side of the wide, marshy swamp, the smoldering remains of a campfire sent tendrils of smoke into the jungle's canopy. The boy stood holding the dog by the scruff of its neck. He looked as if he wanted to eat Barnacle. Or me. Without breaking eye contact, he jerked a spear from the ground, one of several stabbed into the mud.

I could have run, but instead hesitated. He was just a boy, after all. Couldn't have been more than seven or eight. *How accurate can he be from that distance?* Thing is, I didn't really want to find out, so I stopped hesitating and turned to run back the way I'd come.

Only at that exact moment something coiled around my ankle, clamped down, and … lifted me off the ground.

The spring-rope trap yanked me up, swinging wildly as it flung me over the wide, marshy swamp choked with lily pads, saw grass, and tall reeds. I bounced up and down like you see people do when they bungee jump, my head skimming the inky black water. At that exact moment my face settled a foot or so above a long spiked tail that thrashed beneath me. Finding an alligator circling beneath me was pretty much the only thing that could have made my situation worse. The alligator hissed, its jaws snapping at my dangling hair. I don't mind telling you, I was pretty scared. And not only because of the alligator. Snakes glided across the water. So falling in definitely was not something I was going to want to do.

Rebecca screamed. I jerked, looked up and back, and saw her on the mushy bank where I'd been standing moments earlier. Unlike me, she did not have her foot in the loop of a rope-spring trap.

What she did have wrapped around her instead was a large, black arm clamped tightly around her waist. Behind her stood what I assumed was the tribal chief. With ease he hauled her into the swamp and waded out until the water was above his waist. For a moment I was afraid he planned to drown her but he continued on until the pair reached a marshy mudflat not more than a few yards wide. Bleached bones lay scattered about on the matted grass. She fought to get free, but he was too big and strong. Not that getting free would have helped her much. The snakes had left me and were swimming towards the marshy mudflat. So escaping back into the water wasn't really a great option.

The chief lashed Rebecca's wrists and ankles with ropes and pulled them tight, then he looped the other ends around bamboo stakes. Her body made a small X on the gator nest.

Grunting a grunt that sounded like a grunt of satisfaction, the chief waded back into the black water. The alligator stopped circling beneath me. Flicking its tail several times, the gator dove under and disappeared for, like, several seconds. I hoped it was going after the chief, but as I'm sure you have guessed, our luck at that point was of the bad kind. The chief waded out, shook himself the way a black lab will, and disappeared into the jungle.

The alligator sprang from the water and charged up the marshy mudflat towards Rebecca.

CHAPTER 19

REBECCA, THE GATOR AND THE SNAKE

I expected Rebecca to scream and cry out. I would have. But she kept quiet. So I screamed: "DO NOT MOVE," which was unnecessary since she was staked to the ground. And I encouraged her with words like: "There is an alligator at your feet. And snakes slithering towards you!" Reassuring words like that.

Rebecca lay on her back, eyes focused on the pink clouds banked against the lush green hills above the tropical jungle's lush, green canopy. I think she was in shock. I would have been. I hung by my ankle, dangling dangerously close to the slimy swamp with its mossy reeds and algae blooms. Gnats buzzed my ears. Sweat trickled into my eyes.

Across the way on the muddy bank, still held by his neck, Barnacle squirmed. It seemed every time I turned around the mutt had found another way to endanger my life. If a dog was a man's best friend then the two of us needed couples therapy.

Bare-chested men with oily black skin crowded around the boy and pounded spears and sticks on the ground. Apparently catching a small canine in a jungle was cause for celebration.

I reached with my right hand and felt the curved needle, the only weapon I owned. If I hurried I might be able to cut myself free and swim to Rebecca. I worked my hand all the way into my pocket and … the needle tumbled out, skipping off my chest, its tip narrowly missing my chin.

The shouts of the bare-chested men with oily black skin grew louder. I do not think they were shouts of encouragement.

I contorted my body and tried to pull myself up the way a male gymnast will on the still rings. Bending at the waist with my body taut, I strained until my abdominal muscles screamed. If I could grab the rope there was a chance I could climb up and reach the branch. With a final grunt of effort I reached up. Not even close. I fell back, panting, sweating, thinking: *If I ever get back home, I'm going to spend more time getting into shape.*

"Ricky!"

The gator emerged from the inky water. Its long, wide body flattened the matted brown grass as it crawled towards Rebecca. She seemed to be trying to kick at the creature, though that was pretty much impossible. I tried for the rope one more time and surprised myself by actually snagging it. Maybe it was adrenaline, I don't know, but using all my strength, I pulled myself upright until I clasped the rope above my head.

"Ricky, do something!"

I guess Rebecca could not see that I *was* doing something. In her defense, she was on her back with an alligator almost on top of her. The thing I was doing was bouncing with the rope. Overhead the tree branch sagged and creaked.

"I am doing something!" I yelled.

"Whatever you are doing, do it faster!"

I took a quick peek in her direction. The gator had competition: a huge snake. If there were a sports league for snakes this one would have been the Shaquille O'Neal of snakes.

Shaquille O'Neal the snake slithered over Rebecca's knee, then up and over her thigh, across a part of her body I will not mention, and then its head disappeared into her blouse. Horrified, I watched as its squirming rope-like body moved under her clothing. When its huge viper head finally emerged near her throat, Rebecca shrieked so loudly the snake recoiled as if to strike.

Rebecca stopped shrieking. To be honest, I think she fainted. I would have.

Right then the limb above me creaked. I jumped faster.

As if things were not scary enough, the alligator opened its massive jaws and hissed. At Rebecca or Shaquille O'Neal the snake, I wasn't sure.

Apparently Shaquille O'Neal the snake was none too happy to have competition. Shaq struck, sinking its fangs into the gator's tough hide. For a few seconds the two reptiles rolled onto and over Rebecca, snapping and thrashing and hissing.

I jumped some more, the limb creaked some more, and then, taking a deep breath, I leaned back, looked up at the jungle's green canopy, and fell, plunging toward the water the way cliff divers do.

My hair brushed the water, the rope stretched, the tips of my ears went under and … the rope began to pull me back up.

SNAP!

The limb broke. I fell into the inky water.

Right then the huge limb crashed down on top of me, driving me deeper. It took me like half a minute of fumbling with the rope around my ankle to realize I would never work

it free. So I swam for the surface. Only the weight of the tree branch pulled me back down. I yanked and tugged and, with the rope still attached to my ankle and the tree branch attached to the rope, I clawed my way up and gulped air, then looked for Rebecca.

She was gone. Or rather I was gone. The stream's current was carrying me downstream into the dense dark jungle.

If you're looking for a hero in this story, look elsewhere.

Exhausted, I lay back in the water, clasped my hands behind my head, and floated away, all the while trying not to think about Rebecca, the gator, and Shaquille O'Neal the snake.

CHAPTER 20

THE GROG SHOP

My thinking was this: the stream would lead to a river that would take me to the sea and the sea was where the schooner should be. If I couldn't save Rebecca, I could at least let the schooner's skipper know that she would not be needing his services.

Up to that point I had lost a girl who quite possibly was the time-slip equivalent of my high school crush, and a dog that quite possibly held the key to finding some long lost pirate treasure, my dead dad, and my way home.

So things were not all that great in pirate land.

The river was dark and deep. The jungle was simply dark. I don't need to tell you that I was more than a little concerned. But as it happened, for once my not-so-great plan worked; the river dumped me into a bay. I swam to shore and lugged my tree branch onto a beach. In the harbor large ships lay at

anchor, their dark hulls reflecting the moon's light. In one corner of the beach, two fishermen pulled a skiff onto the sand and left it next to other smaller boats painted blue and yellow and green. On the waterfront street, carts loaded with sacks being offloaded onto ships docked on a long wharf.

In the moon's light I finally freed my ankle from the rope. I don't mind telling you, I was one happily liberated young man. Which meant I felt the need to celebrate. And by celebrate I mean, drink fresh water. Problem was, there were no water fountains in the waterfront public park. In fact, there was no waterfront public park.

So I went in search of a grog shop.

Hopping over a low stone seawall I made my way towards the back alleys. In pirate movies, back alleys are always where you find bloodthirsty men, and in general, thirsty men. And where you find thirsty men, you will generally find men who sail schooners and other ships.

Swarthy fellows leaned against doorframes and porch posts. Bales of cotton and casks of rum filled the loading dock of a large warehouse. A pair of menacing individuals began to walk toward me, one with a machete in his hand. I darted up a side street, turned right, and found myself on a bustling lane. Pennants fluttered over doors, marking the loyalties of business owners. Spanish and Dutch, British and Portuguese. I took careful note of the stenciled icons, and guessed the store types: seamstress shop, tea room, shoe cobbler. No grog shop.

At the end of the block I found a dirt path running along a picket fence and followed the trail until it ended abruptly in a thicket of vines. The stench of rum hung in the air, which let me know I was getting close to my prize. Empty bottles and shards of broken glass littered the ground. I peered through the brush and saw a small door marking the entrance to a stone hut. Nailed above the threshold was a hand-lettered sign that read, "Splice the Main, Ye Sandy Bottom Gulls and Bouys. We

Got Yer Gulpers, Nippers, and PainKillers" In smaller lettering, "Bob's-a-dying so Weepers welcome ever' Wednesday. Two-For-One Deals."

Whoever Bob was, he sounded like the kind of fellow who might know where I would find the skipper of a schooner. I pushed my way through the briars and banged on the door.

A wooden flap slid open. In the slot a yellow eye appeared. "State your business."

"Looking for a captain."

"Covers a mighty wide swath of canvas. What be yer cap'n's name?"

"Commands a ship bound for Port Charles."

The flap slammed shut. I waited. And waited. I knocked again.

The door opened a few inches. A weasel-faced man with a scar on his cheek peered out. "State your business."

"I'm here to see the captain of a ship bound for Port Charles."

"Cap'n Desmond?"

"I ... ah ... yes, that's him."

"Wait here."

The door closed. I waited. And waited. The pair from earlier, one of which still carried his machete, pushed past me, knocked, and was welcomed in. The door shut, leaving me alone in the alley.

I knocked again.

The door cracked open. A bald man with no neck glared at me. "State your business."

Sighing loudly, I said, "I'm looking for ..."

"... A ship bound for Port Charles, that much I know."

"So why ask?"

"Can ne'er be too careful." He yanked me inside and slammed the door shut behind. Lanterns hung from low ceiling beams, casting a yellow glow through the haze of smoke. With the stink of tobacco and rum on his breath, the bald-headed man growled, "The cap'n has been waitin' fer ye." He shoved me toward a back room separated by a beaded curtain. As we walked past, chair legs scraped against the hardwood floor; men turned to stare. All talking and loud laughing ceased.

"Wait here."

I waited. In my short time at the grog shop I had become an excellent waiter.

The bald-headed man leaned into the beaded curtain and said loud enough for me to hear, "Lad here says he's got business in Port Charles."

"D-does he now?" a voice replied. "Well, h-h-have him join us."

I'm sure I do not need to tell you that the man's stuttering voice did not leave me with a good feeling.

Chapter 21

With pirate friends like these, who needs sharks?

The bald-headed man pushed me through the beaded curtain and into a small, crowded room that had the aromatic fragrance of unwashed men.

Turtle Bill sat across a table from LaFoote, who sat studying a map that covered nearly the entire table. With one hand the pirate captain moved a candle over the chart, his eyes fixed on the crude drawing of mountains and rivers.

"Sit!" he said, without looking up.

Without waiting to be he hit or shot or cut, Turtle Bill vacated the chair and joined the other smelly pirates who stood around the table.

The straight-back wooden chair creaked under my weight. A man—who I assumed was drunk, us being in a grog shop and all—rested his head on his forearm. The drunk stirred when I pulled my chair back, lifted his face towards me, and stared through slitted eyes. His saffron nose was swollen and bent, lower lip crusted over with blood. A weak smile exposed pink teeth from bloody gums.

"Good to see you, son." I struggled to hear the doctor's wheezing words over the den of noise outside our small room.

"The good doctor will not be good fer long if he doesn't tell me what I want to know," said LaFoote, pounding the map with his fist. "Where is it?" he asked me.

With my gaze fixed on the doctor, I replied, "Where's what?"

"You know, the dog."

"What dog?"

"Don't toy with me, boy. I'll cut out yer tongue and sell it fer sausage, I will."

"Captain knows," said the doctor.

"He ran off," I said. "Some natives have him. Or did. They may be having mutt for dinner about now."

"Ye mean mutton."

"No, just mutt."

"And the girl?"

"Girl?"

"I swear, boy. Seems ter me ye got a hearing problem. I can fix that fast enough, though. Stab this dirk in yer ears and make them holes bigger. THE SQUIRE'S NIECE, WHERE IS SHE?"

"I'm … not exactly sure."

LaFoote snatched a knife from his belt and, tilting the doctor's chin upwards, placed the blade against his throat, sawing back and forth as if carving a ham. "Ever seen a man try to breathe with his throat slit? Gruesome business. Each time he inhales he blows tiny pink bubbles. Gurgles when he tries to talk. Takes a long time fer him to choke on his blood, it does. Now tell me plain: WHERE IS THE GIRL AND DOG?"

"I swear, I don't know. In the jungle back—"

LaFoote's blade sliced deeper; blood sputtered out of the doctor's throat.

"In a swamp! She and the dog, middle of the island. But I'm not sure I can find my way back. Besides, both are probably dead by now."

"Oh, ye'll find the dog, ye will. Of that ye can be sure." LaFoote put the knife away. "And ye best pray he be not dead."

CHAPTER 22

DEAD LOW TIDE

The moon was full and high by the time we reached the wide delta where the swamp's river emptied into the sea. The *Black Avenger* lay anchored far behind us in the large harbor framed on three sides by hills shaped like tall cone hats. "Witches' peaks," LaFoote had called them. Voices echoed across the water as the men aboard the ship jeered, drank, and fought. We left a small garrison ashore and pushed off in a gig. Then we paddled into the swamp, navigating the maze of mangrove trees. I knelt on my knees in the center of the gig, hands bound behind my back, and feet, too. Fish jumped, bugs bit.

I sulked.

It wouldn't matter if I found the dog or not. LaFoote would kill me as soon as he had Barnacle and if I couldn't locate the mangy mutt, he would kill me anyway. So basically I was a dead man either way.

The doctor had told LaFoote about the longitude and latitude tattooed on Barnacle's belly; that seemed obvious enough. So I was not having what you would call a great ending to my first Christmas vacation day in the Caribbean. It was coming up on twenty-four hours since I'd placed my bag of popcorn in the microwave and torched our apartment and apartment building. Mom was home by now, I was sure of it. Someone would have called to let her know about the fire.

I'd described the swamp and natives to LaFoote as best I could. I even marked on the map where I thought I'd been captured. LaFoote stood in the front of the canoe, his large frame bent slightly forward as he scanned the water ahead. Every few seconds he'd order the oarsmen to correct their course. With one shove I could have sent him tumbling out of the gig, but I didn't dare chance it. Not with pirates sitting in front of, beside, and behind me.

The maze grew tighter, the stream we navigated narrower. No one spoke. Only the sound of paddles striking the water interrupted the buzzing of mosquitoes chewing on my neck and ears. Finally the gig rounded a sharp bend and glided into the wide, marshy swamp. A thumbnail of black mud lay ahead near the charred stones of a campfire I'd spied earlier. Scorched logs lay scattered about near the water's edge. Palm branches stood in a pile, fuel for the fire. The canoe pushed onto mud and stuck fast.

"Skinny Bob. This boy'll need a leash if he's ter go fer a hike in the jungle."

"I smell shrimp on the barbie," said Skinny Bob, making a mock show of sniffing my neck.

"It's your upper lip," I said.

Skinny Bob peered down his nose and sniffed again, then whacked me on the back of the head. "Shut up, shrimp." Skinny Bob threaded a short rope through the bindings around my wrists and gave it a tug, nearly pulling me out of the gig.

"Loosen them bindings so he can walk," LaFoote ordered. "But not ter much. Don' want him ter get ideas."

Skinny Bob knelt down, a considerable feat given his size, and adjusted the crude shackles around my ankles. "Tied tighter than the Queen's corset in all the right places, he is, Cap'n." Skinny Bob patted me unnecessarily hard on the cheek. "Return to me soon, love."

"Ricky? Ricky, is that you?" a voice called.

The familiar voice caused my heart to skip. *She's not dead.* I strained to see across the swamp at the matted gator nest. A dark log appeared to be partially buried at the water's edge.

Jumping to my feet, I stepped from the gig to go to Rebecca. "You okay? Don't move, I'll be right there." Before I could take a second step, Skinny Bob's fist hammered the back of my head, knocking me into the water.

With my face under water Skinny Bob yanked me up and, still holding me by the hair, flung me up the slope to where LaFoote and his men waited.

"Don't worry," I called back to Rebecca. "Soon as I find the dog I'll come back for you."

It was a lie, of course. LaFoote would never simply let me return to the swamp, but I had to say something.

"But the dog, he's …" I held my breath, hoping she wasn't about to blurt out *DEAD!*

"Run off," I volunteered, "I know. But I'll find him, don't you worry."

I knew no such thing.

"But how *could* you know," she replied. "You fell in before those savage men …"

"I just know."

Not really, I thought. Except unless Rebecca was going along with the con, which I did not think was possible, the dog had run off. Which meant he might still be alive. Which meant if I could get Barnacle first and figure out what the special, secret password was, I could get back to Mom and Quiet Cove.

So that was my plan: find the dog, figure out how to talk to it, and POOF, just like Dorothy I would return home.

Rebecca strained the cords on her neck to lift and pivot her head. Her eyes glistened in the moonlight, mouth curved up into a half smile. "Ricky, please …" Her voice cracked. "Hurry."

LaFoote said, "Longer ye keep yapping, Barbeque, less time that prissy-pants lass has before the water covers her."

LaFoote took my leash and started toward the jungle, pulling me along behind. "Bob, ye stay here with the girl. Enjoy yerself if ye like, but don' mark her. Now that I know the Squire's nephew is a lass, she be worth more. Men in port pay extra fer the young ones." Addressing the other men in the gig, he said, "Rest of ya, paddle back ter the ship and tell the others to make ready to sail. Two Pin Jim, ye come with me."

"Chin up," I called to Rebecca. It was my weak attempt at encouragement.

"What does 'chin up' mean, boss?" asked Two Pin Jim.

LaFoote studied Two Pin Jim as though realizing for the first time that the man might be too stupid to spell I.Q. "It means, the lass is ter keep her spirits up 'cause the boy here thinks he can save her. Which he can't. And if ye don't shut up and stop asking dumb questions I'll have ye keelhauled."

"Got it, boss."

A cloud passed across the moon, turning the swamp dark. Small waves lapped against the mud. Water pooled around Rebecca's thighs, rushing up and past her waist. Taking a long final look at the girl I could not save, I turned away and started into the jungle.

We'd only gone a short ways when I heard Rebecca scream. Which meant Skinny Bob was passing the time by taking pleasures with her. I walked faster, stumbling over roots and tramping down dense underbrush. At last her cries fell away, leaving only the night sounds of the jungle and the steady thumping of my own heart breaking.

CHAPTER 23

"DOGGED" BY REGRETS

My plan for finding the dog stank. So did everything else about our hike into the jungle: rotting trees, smelly soil, Two Pin Jim and his strong exhaust. (Note to self: Don't walk downwind of a pirate who's had turtle soup for dinner.)

Our walk through the jungle took on a solemn mood. The soil seeped through my toes; each time I stepped I heard a sucking sound. Large branches knitted a leafy canopy overhead, blocking out the moon's light. At first I tried to watch where I placed my bare feet, hoping to avoid logs, roots, and snakes .... The tip of LaFoote's cutlass hurried me along.

"So ... the dog," I said in a feeble attempt to walk slower. "Thought you tossed him overboard."

"Shut up."

"But I thought he was dead, that your crew threw him over?"

"Won't work."

"What won't work?"

"Ye talking while walking so ye can find a way to run off."

That absolutely was my plan. "You think that dog is worth all this effort?"

"Me? No. But the boys wanted a night in port ter let off steam and I figured as long as we was on the island, I may as well hunt fer the dog. In case, ye know, the legend is true."

"There's a legend?"

"Ye know there is."

"Tell me about the legend."

"The legend what says the dog can lead a body to booty."

"By the way, I've been meaning to ask," I said. "How come they call a treasure booty?"

"Shut up."

Leaves rustled, limbs creaked. Far away I heard the crash of waves breaking on shore. We were getting farther from Rebecca and Skinny Bob.

"How *did* you escape those British warships?"

Whack! "Told ye ter shut up."

"Warn't hard," said Two Pin Jim. "The cap'n here, he ..."

"No talking ter the prisoner, Jim."

"Aye, Cap'n." Two Pin Jim hurried up beside me. We walked in silence for several steps before he whispered to me, "See, once we was clear of that channel —"

Whack! "Told ye to keep quiet."

"No you didn't, boss. You said no talking to the prisoner."

"Same difference."

"But, Cap'n, it's a good story. 'Sides, the lad ain't gonna live long enough to do us no harm."

"Good point."

"We lured the warship into the shallows," Two Pin Jim said, "making like we had run aground and was sinking. Then when the skipper of that warship presented his broadsides, the cap'n ordered the crew to give 'em a bang."

"The recoil of the cannons pushed the man-of-war's keel onto the reef," LaFoote said, joining in on the telling of the tale. "From there she was an easy mark."

"And the rest of the fleet?" I asked.

"Ah, that's where that young lass back in the swamp did us a service," LaFoote continued. "Them kegs of gunpowder that ye blowed up next ter that frigate left the water full of debris. The fleet slowed to look for survivors. By the time the smoke cleared we were leagues away. But ye know all this and more," LaFoote said in a not-so-nice way that suggested we both knew I had seen him kill the Squire in the treasure storage room.

"Cap'n here sailed over the horizon, then circled back and come in around the east end of Santa Maria so as not to be seen by any of them warships," said Two Pin Jim. 'He reckoned ye and the girl would be looking for a ship to take ya to her daddy so he tells the crew to spread out and watch the pubs. Find ye and the lass and I find the mutt."

"Ye made it too easy, Barbeque. But then yer are a brash buck with more starch than sense. Didn't take more than a couple of lashes with Skinny Bob's whip to get the truth about the dog out of the good doctor."

We came to a wide area of tidal flats covered in reeds. "I could find the dog faster if you untied my feet."

"And run faster, no doubt. Ye got all the rope yer gonna get."

Animal sounds filled the jungle. The roaring of waves crashing became louder. Far away savages beat their drums. I took some comfort knowing that Rebecca wasn't with them, though Skinny Bob's company was not much better.

"How long do you think it'll be before those warships realize you've doubled back?" I asked. "You anchored the *Black Avenger* in plain sight. As soon as they sail past the harbor entrance, they'll capture your crew. Then where will you be? Up a creek, is where."

I was hoping to rattle him. It did not work: at least not on LaFoote.

"Makes a good point, Cap'n."

"Shut up, Jim."

To make myself sound even dumber, which at that point was not easy, I said, "Dog's probably dead, anyway. Judging from the looks of those spear-throwing savages, I think they were planning on grilling hot dogs."

Two Pin Jim stifled a chuckle. "Get it, Cap'n? Hot dog?"

"Jim, I swear. One more word out of ye and ye will be the one turning on the spit."

"Doggone shame he got away like he did," I continued. Two Pin Jim clamped his hand over his mouth; his shoulders shook. "That mutt's probably sniffing around, looking for the man who shot his paw."

Tears rolled down Two Pin Jim's cheeks.

"Why, I wouldn't be surprised if that mutt isn't dog-tired and—"

LaFoote raised his fist as if to smack me. "Shut up, both of ye!"

"You think hitting solves everything, don't you?"

"Reckon it worked well enough on the doctor."

Wind rattled branches, reeds rustled. I don't want to keep bringing this up, but my ankles were killing me, my back burned from sunburn, and my backside stung from being popped with wet towels.

"It's not my dog," I said. "He's a stray. If you want to catch him we'll all three need to fan out."

LaFoote stroked his beard as if considering my explanation. "Jim, untie that rope from around his legs."

"But Cap'n, he's tricking us."

"As long as Skinny Bob has the lass he'll do as I say, ain't that right?"

I nodded. Two Pin Jim loosened the knot.

LaFoote leaned close. "Ye listen and listen good, Barbeque. I mean to get me that treasure what be marked on that dog's belly. Ye can either find that dog and save the girl, or run. Run and ye both die. Find the dog and it be only ye that I kill."

"You'll let her go if I find the mutt?"

"I got no quarrel with the governor's daughter. No point sailing into a squall unless ye have ter. Ye, on the other hand, yer just extra weight. Ballast, as it were, to be tossed overboard."

I said nothing, only watched as Two Pin removed the rope from my ankles. Now that I could walk, there was a measure of hope. I bent down, massaging my lower calves. Between the coarse rope and iron shackles, the skin above my feet looked like raw bacon. "I'm not running, let's be clear about that. But try to keep up."

Over the creek and through the woods I walked quickly. It was like we were running to Grandmother's house. Only unlike the horse in that song, I was not feeling very good about my prospects of finding the dog and my way back home. This not-so-good feeling lasted maybe one and a half seconds. Which is how long it took me to notice that we had reached a sheer rock face covered with thick vines and a dead end. Which meant my not-so-good feeling turned into a really bad feeling. I was about to suggest we turn back when I looked up and saw, about thirty feet overhead, a wide ledge.

"This way," I said. Carefully, I eased sideways and, holding on to one of the creepers, pulled myself up, toes digging into the cracks as I scaled the cliff.

LaFoote struggled to do the same. His boots and the heavy layers of clothing weighed him down. Sword and hardware clanked and his grunting grew louder. Two Pin Jim yelled for us to *hold up;* I pressed on. If you think about it, scaling a cliff is pretty dumb, but boys do dumb stuff all the time. Like climb trees, for example. I mean, it only takes one rotten branch to send you to the hospital with a broken arm, but boys never think about stuff like that. Mom told me one time, on a day when I had done something dumber than normal, that a boy's brain doesn't fully develop until he's twenty-five. "That's when he starts acting like he's got some common sense," she said. "With girls it's closer to twenty-one. I pray every day, Ricky, that you live long enough to have all your wires connected."

What Mom told me explains a lot. Like why the age for joining the military is eighteen, but the drinking age is twenty-one. Apparently boys don't think they'll be the one who gets shot but they can't wait to down shots.

I reached the summit. Far below us on the other side of the ridge, church bells chimed, dogs barked. A donkey brayed, suggesting a farm nearby. The smell of salt and sea rushed up the hillside. Beyond the grassy meadow before us, lanterns flickered as people walked about in a village.

At last LaFoote flung himself over the ledge. "See the ..." he rolled onto his back and, breathing heavy, said, "... dog?"

I know what you're thinking. (Not really; that's just something people say.) You're thinking why didn't I snatch the dirk from LaFoote's belt right then and stab him in his chest. I'll tell you why I didn't: because for the most part the average person isn't that ruthless. Sure, in a fit of rage someone might grab a knife and stab someone. Stuff like that happens. But if the average person is in their right mind they'll think about the consequences of trying ... and missing ... and decide against doing something so stupid. Even if you succeed in killing the person, there are the media and court dates and legal fees and you never really ever get your life back. Better to turn the other cheek, as it were, slip away, and let fate deal with the bad person.

At least that's what I was thinking at that moment.

I pointed toward an iron fence on the far side of the grassy meadow. A large-winged creature came gliding overhead, making a slow, lazy circle above the rows of headstones. The black vulture settled onto a gnarled branch of a large tree. Here I should point out that moment I realized the grassy meadow was a graveyard. My thinking was this: If I were a dog, I would hide in a graveyard.

Two Pin Jim bent forward, hands on his knees.

"On yer feet, Jim," LaFoote said. "No time ter rest."

"Two of you go on," Two Pin Jim said, panting. "I'll keep watch."

"Fer what?" said LaFoote. "Shooting stars?

"Lemme be for a few, Cap'n. Two of you sing out if you see something."

"'Fraid of ghosts, are ye, Jim?"

"Me auntie, when I was a wee boy, she said I was not to disturb the dead."

"And I suppose yer auntie be paying yer wages?"

"No, Cap'n, but when it comes to disrespecting dead folks she —"

LaFoote pulled his sword and placed the blade against Jim's neck. "Disrespecting the dead, says ye. Perhaps ye'd like ter join them."

"Don't 'spose it'd hurt to look," Jim said, straightening.

I ambled over to a headstone and looked behind it. No dog. I led the pair through the meadow, pausing when we reached the entrance to the cemetery. A wooden sign warned:

No Trespassing!

Vandals and "spooks" that means you!

Two Pin Jim bent forward as though trying to read the sign. "What's it say?"

I squinted. "Thursday nights two-for-one rum shots. All the squid you can eat." There was no point scaring the poor pirate without reason.

"Don't like squid. Gives me the trots."

LaFoote boxed Jim's ear. "Yeh dim-witted conch chowder. Boy be messing with ye. The sign says keep out."

"Good idea," said Jim, backing away.

WHACK! "Get ter looking fer that mutt!"

I knew from my world history studies, and from a few Easter service sermons, that not everyone could afford a proper burial. I figured a potter's field, outside of town and downwind of the prevailing breeze, would be a good place to bury the poor. All I had to do was find the graveyard's cave where they tossed in the corpses of the criminals and vagrants.

Bats gave away its location. They were leaving on their evening rounds, darting out and zipping away like dark dots. Hundreds of them, flying up into the night sky.

I pointed at the jumble of boulders gathered against the slope of the meadow. "There."

"There?" said LaFoote?

"A tomb. Large one, I bet."

Not really. It was only some rocks with a small opening in the center, but I felt certain that if the graveyard had a cave for corpses, that would be the place for it.

"If the dog is around, he'll be in there gnawing on a bone."

"In that case, ye best go see," LaFoote said to me. "Jim, ye go in there with him."

In case you're wondering, I did not like the sound of that.

"But Cap'n, a tomb?"

WHACK! WHACK!

"Both of ye, crawl inter that hole and see if the dog be in there."

Which of course I did.

And that's when my Caribbean pirate adventure turned really scary.

CHAPTER 24

BONE-TIRED

A wild tangle of vines covered the cave-tomb's opening. As we approached I heard a swishing coming from inside, as if someone were sweeping a broom. At the sound of guttural, gurgling, snarling, I stopped. The commotion inside did not sound inviting.

LaFoote peered into the small, fang-shaped hole. As I said, vines covered most of the opening so he could not see too far in.

"Ye sure the dog's in that cave?"

"No. But if they toss the poor in and let them rot, then I bet there are plenty of bones to gnaw."

The snapping and snarling coming from inside the tomb increased.

"Don't like the sounds of that, Cap'n. Remember how on Devil's Back Bay, Skinny Bob found that rum distillery with all them bats. Bit some of the crew, they did."

"Hush, you imbecile. I'm trying ter think."

Two Pin Jim leaned over my shoulder and in a hushed voice said, "One of 'em gave Skinny Bob a nasty bite. For nearly a week Cap'n had to keep 'im tied to the mast on account of he was frothing at the mouth and talking gibberish."

"By thunder, Jim, if ye don't furl that flapping tongue of yers I'll shove ye in that cave myself."

"Yes, Cap'n."

LaFoote stepped closer, swinging his cutlass as he hacked at vines.

"Saw visions too, he did," added Jim. "Kept screaming jellyfish was crawling up his legs and arms."

"Jim, I swear!"

"Sorry, Cap'n." In a nearly silent somber voice: "Bob's never been right since."

"Is that why he's, you know, such a bully?"

"Was like that when he come aboard. Dropped on his head when he was just a little feller and loosened some planks, I think."

Dropping onto all fours, LaFoote peered inside.

"So ... How'd you get a name like Two Pin?" I said.

"Coconut billiards."

"Never heard of it."

"Ya stand ten rum jugs up on end in sort of a diamond shape and then roll a coconut towards 'em. Man who knocks down the most jugs wins."

"But doesn't the first guy have the advantage? I mean, he could bowl them all over with the first throw."

"Don't hardly ever happen. Most only knock over a few, usually, on account of they're still filled with rum. And for each jug ya knock over ya have ter take a swig. Crowd finishes off the rest. Can take a while 'fore the second feller gets a go."

"Still doesn't explain the name."

"We call them jugs 'pins' and I'm real good at collecting a 'split.' A split is —"

"I know. Two jugs on opposite sides of the lane."

"So you play?"

A short yelp came from inside the cave. LaFoote stood quickly, pointing inside, and gave my leash a tug. "Fetch him."

I had no idea if the dog was in the cave or not. Didn't matter. All I needed was to get free of LaFoote. I knew he wouldn't let go of my rope but that was okay. I only needed a few minutes to explore the cave. Once inside I hoped to find a second exit. Most tombs have a secret, second outlet. Least, they do on Tomb Raider.

I tramped through the bushes and knelt as if to crawl in.

"Not you, boy." LaFoote jerked me up. He stepped back so Jim could pass. "He'll go."

"But Cap'n. I don't want to get bit by a bat like Skinny Bob. 'Sides, that dog don't sound all that friendly. Let me fire a round in there and see can I flush him out."

"And draw down a garrison of soldiers on us?" LaFoote kicked Two Pin Jim in the seat of his trousers and sent him stumbling toward the cave's entrance. "Now quit your whining and bring me that dog."

Mumbling under his breath about how bats "can make a body howl at the moon," Two Pin Jim dropped to his belly and began slithering between the two fang-shaped rocks that covered the entrance. Soon only the muddy backside of his trousers remained visible in the pale moonlight.

"Best hope that's your dog, Barbeque. A rising tide sinks all boats."

I said nothing. I think what he was hinting at was that Rebecca would be nearly out of time, by now. Assuming Skinny Bob had not freed her from the mudflat.

I casually eyed the knives and pistols on LaFoote's belt.

"Try it," he said, tracking my gaze. "I dare ye."

From inside the cave came snarling and cursing.

"Cap'n. There's something in here, all right, but it ain't no dog, it's—"

There came a loud hissing, like a steam valve giving way, followed by what I was sure were jaws snapping shut. Two Pin Jim screamed and the tips of his toes bounced off dirt. With his left heel Two Pin Jim tried to hook the edge of the fanged rocks to keep from being pulled in but missed. He shrieked again but this time his cry was followed by a slobbering, chewing noise from the thing that had hold of him. Bones snapped, Jim moaned, and the creature dragged the poor pirate into the cave.

"That ain't no dog," said LaFoote, backing away.

I looked at the rope, but I hesitated. I was scared if I tried to run LaFoote would shoot me.

Two Pin Jim shrieked again, only this time his cry had a sucking, wheezing sound. Meanwhile the creature inside the cave made a slobbering, chewing noise.

"Best go check on Jim ter see if he's alive." LaFoote untied my wrists and removed the leash. "In ye go, boy."

"I would rather not."

"It were not a suggestion, Barbeque."

And with that not-so-great-news, I poked my head into the fang-shaped opening and crawled forward.

CHAPTER 25

A MESSAGE FROM THE GRAVE

My plan to escape worked. I was free of the bindings on my ankles and wrists and leash. Free to run back and help Rebecca. Only problem was this: I was in a tomb with a giant man-eating lizard. In case there was any question as to the dietary preferences of the gargantuan creature that lived inside the tomb, it shook its head and in doing so, waggled the bottom half of Two Pin Jim. It was sort of like that scene in Jaws when the big shark bites Quint in half, only from my perspective it was a lot worse because: a) I was, like, three feet from a huge reptile that was at least as big as the shark in Jaws and b) LaFoote threatened to hack me into itty-bitty pieces with an ax he'd found hidden in vines if I did not come out with the dog or Two Pin Jim.

So that was a problem.

"Nice lizard," I said to the humongous sumo-wrestler-Komodo dragon. "Please don't eat me." The oversized gecko continued chomping and chewing on Two Pin Jim who, at that point, had become One Pin Jim.

If you have never spent any time around lizards—and why would anyone want to spend time around lizards—you may not realize how lethargic lizards are. When I was small Mom used to read me a book about nature and one of the pages had the words, "Lazy as a lizard." That pretty much sums up the energy level of your average oversized, man-eating iguana. Which worked to my advantage because, like I said, with LaFoote threatening to make chopped barbeque with the ax he'd found, I went exploring for the backdoor escape that I was sure existed.

In doing so I discovered the tomb was much larger than it first appeared. Huge, in fact, and it extended back into the hillside like some mausoleums you see in old cemeteries. (Here I am thinking of the Hollywood Cemetery in Richmond where Confederate soldiers are buried, as is former Confederate President Jefferson Davis.) Below is a drawing of some skulls on shelves I found. The tomb wasn't nearly this organized or nice but you get the general idea.

You want to know what else I found?

Barnacle. If you are thinking he was dead or had been chewed up by the giant lizard, you would be wrong. The sorry mutt was very much alive. Scared, but alive. He had taken cover behind a row of skulls and was cowering out of sight.

Here is something else I found: a headstone that for some reason lay in a corner of the tomb along with some other headstones that were chipped and broken and to all appearances headed for the trash heap. Except they were in the tomb with Godzilla, king of the lizard monsters, so there was not much chance any graveyard caretaker would be along to remove them anytime soon. Here are a few of the headstone sayings I found.

Here lies the body of old man Peas,
buried beneath the flowers and trees,
but Peas ain't here, just the pod,
Peas shucked out and went to God.

Stop talking! I'm trying to sleep.

I took a wrong turn. Do NOT follow me.

Forgive me, Ricky. Find me and forgive
me before it's too late.
Richard Justice Bradshaw

You know what's weird? I'll tell you what's weird. My dad's name is Richard Justice Bradshaw. Seeing the headstone somehow impressed upon me the urgency of grabbing the dog and getting the out of the tomb.

"If you don't want to come out from behind that skull, I understand," I said to Barnacle. "If I were a dog I would stay hidden."

Kicking aside a few of the skulls, I eased towards the mutt. As bones scrapped against stones and dirt, a low, rumbling snarl met my ears. Out of the corner of my eye I saw Godzilla swish its tail, gulping down another few inches of One Pin Jim, who now was more like Half Pin Jim.

"See that oversized gecko?" I said to Barnacle. "Once he's finished eating that poor pirate he'll come for me. Or you. We need to leave."

Somehow me talking nicely to the dog helped calm him. The tip of his tail wagged a little. Reaching out, I scooped him into my arms. As I cradled him close to my chest, Barnacle's hot, smelly breath warmed my neck. My fingers found the top of his head and, cupping my hand over his eyes, I scratched his ears. Basically I was trying to keep him calm while I searched the back of the tomb for a way out.

"AWFUL QUIET IN THERE!" LaFoote bellowed. "YOU FIND THAT DOG YET?"

The human garbage disposal lizard stopped chomping and hissed, blowing a big lizard snot bubble from one of its nostrils.

This caused the dog to jerk, yelp, and jump from my arms, which sent Godzilla into a thrashing, slashing charge at my feet. I screamed, tumbled backwards, tripped over dead people, some still with skin on, and landed on my back. Like before when we were on the beach, the dog began barking at the giant Komodo dragon. You know how some people say that when they were in a really scary situation, they suddenly got clarity and felt calm? That definitely did not happen to me. The only thing I suddenly felt was a strong urge to wet myself. Wriggling and flailing, I untangled myself from the bodies under and around me and pushed myself onto hands and knees.

"SO ... THE DOG IS *IN* THERE," LaFoote roared, in a less-than-pleasant way. "STAND BACK! I'M COMING IN!"

Shoving the ax in front and ahead of him, LaFoote crawled into the tomb far enough to see. At that exact moment, Godzilla whirled, belched, and vomited up Half Pin Jim. I am sure I do not need to describe what that looked and smelled like, so we'll skip that part. What I do need to mention is that right then Godzilla opened its massive, log-moving-size jaws as if to bite off LaFoote's head. But the captain of the *Black Avenger* had other ideas.

Below is a picture of LaFoote swinging the ax at Godzilla the way any skilled pirate would when engaged in mortal combat with a giant lizard.

The tip of the ax went *THUNK* and cleaved in the skull of the reptile. For the next few moments Godzilla whirled, and rolled, and made loud lizard hissing, shrieking sounds: all the while spewing lizard blood over a beige-pink regurgitated mush that was Half Pin Jim. LaFoote kept his distance, as did Barnacle and I.

Finally the lizard collapsed, made gargling, hissing, whizzing, lizard sighs, and died.

LaFoote snatched the dog from between my legs before I could react.

"Tie yer ankles and wrists," LaFoote said to me. "And do it good. If I find any slack, I'll whack off a finger and more."

I'm sure I do not need to tell you what happened next. In case you're wondering, it was not pleasant.

CHAPTER 26

WALKING THE "SKINNY BOB"

T he wooden deck of the *Black Avenger* felt soft and wet beneath my feet. I would have preferred to remain on the sturdy deck, but LaFoote pushed me out and onto a "Skinny Bob" that flexed and shifted like a rotten diving board. That's what the crew called the plank I stood on: a "Skinny Bob." Apparently the super-sized pirate had come up with the pirate diving board idea all by his lonesome.

"Stand still and try not to fall until I push ye," said LaFoote.

It was nearly impossible to keep my balance on the plank. In front of me, fireflies flew among the trees onshore. The crew had moved the *Black Avenger* to a secluded cove, then headed onto the beach for a night of drinking and fighting and sleeping it off. When I stepped from the "Skinny Bob" and hit the water, no one would know except the drunken crew. Well, the crew and Rebecca. But she had problems of her own.

"Please, no," Rebecca said in a hoarse whisper. "Oh God, help me."

I turned toward the sound of her sobs. She stood about an arm's length away from me on a "Skinny Bob." Like me, her ankles were bound, wrists tied tight. Rebecca cradled a cannonball; her eyes glistened, bursting and spilling with tears as she cut her eyes toward me, silently begging me to do something.

"Did he "I said, "... you know?"

"After you left, that brute ..." She closed her eyes momentarily, as if trying to block out the image of Skinny Bob touching her. "I begged him to stop. Told him I would rather die than ...." Her bottom lip trembled. "Please, Ricky, do something."

LaFoote pressed the end of his sword into the small of her back, causing a trickle of blood to stain her blouse. She arched the upper half of her body as if to avoid its piercing tip.

I whispered to Rebecca, "I have a plan."

I did not have a plan. What I had was panic. But Rebecca needed hope and it was easy enough to offer.

LaFoote snapped his fingers; Barnacle came trotting over. "See, Barbeque. The dog and me, we be like shipmates." From his coat pocket the captain slipped the dog a piece of fish. "I scratch the mutt's back, as it were, he scratches mine."

Barnacle wagged his tail. I will just say at this point I was not happy with the dog.

"You need me and the dog," I said. "Her, not so much. Let the girl go."

"This lass sealed her fate when she hoisted her sails alongside yers. A sacrifice isn't a sacrifice unless it costs ye something and the two of ye fell fer the oldest trick in the book."

"What trick is that?" I asked.

"Ye fell fer each other."

"No, I didn't."

I had, sort of. Only I didn't want her to know.

"But the lass did," LaFoote said.

"You like me?" I asked Rebecca.

"Ye crossed swords with the wrong pirate, and now that's gonna cost the lass her life. Two lovebirds dying in each other's arms. It be a love story fer the ages."

Rebecca looked toward me, shuddering, making small sobbing sounds.

"Blow her a kiss, boy. This be the last ye see of her."

"Please, Ricky, do not leave me."

I thought her comment odd and was about to mouth the words, "Don't worry, I won't," when LaFoote shoved his sword hard in her back. Rebecca shrieked and, reacting to the jab, bucked forward. She fell with an ear-piercing scream and splashed into dark water.

She sank from sight and with her my heart fell and broke.

Chapter 27

The End of LaFoote

A smile parted the wiry whiskers on LaFoote's face "Come on, Barbeque. Give it a go. I know ye want ter take a swing at me." He thrust out his jaw, mocking me, weaving and bobbing like a boxer.

He was right: I wanted to kill him. But with my wrists tied and me still holding a cannonball, whirling and hitting the pirate wasn't really an option. If I whirled and swung, I would have probably dropped the cannonball on my foot.

But then something happened: something odd and miraculous. LaFoote tripped and stumbled and lunged onto the "Skinny Bob." I had not noticed the mysterious man sneaking up from behind. Using the wide end of a boat oar, he clubbed LaFoote a second time on the back of the head. LaFoote's eyes grew wide and with arms spinning paddlewheel-like, he tried to right himself, but his momentum carried him forward.

Twisting, he fell, legs kicking as his black cape fluttered up and over his head. The captain of the *Avenger* hit the water with a huge splash and sank near where Rebecca had gone in.

Stunned, I twisted around, expecting to get clubbed myself, but instead the shadowy figure dropped the paddle, whipped out a long knife, and … cut the rope around my wrists, then my ankles.

"W-w-well," said Turtle Bill. "Ya g-g-gonna save the lass ya love, or not?"

And before I could ask why he was helping me, the first mate gave me a hard shove.

I still held the cannonball when I hit the water.

CHAPTER 28

SECOND CHANCES, OLD ROMANCES

The water's depth was probably twenty feet beneath the ship's keel. In falling, we had landed on the edge of the shore's sloping, sandy beach. Which meant in the moon's light I could make out the shape of Rebecca lying on her side. The cannonball had taken me down quickly. I dropped it and swam to her.

Silk hair shrouded her forehead. Lips dark and parted, eyes shut.

From behind I slipped my hands under her arms and locked my fingers across her chest the way they teach you in lifeguard training. Hugging her tight, I pushed off the bottom with a pair of legs that felt like two large, waterlogged dock pilings. Salt water spilled into my throat; the ship's huge shadow seemed far, far above. Already I was out of air and we were still pretty much on the bottom. I had a long way to go.

We weren't going to make it.

Only I had no choice but to make it. *Focus and kick, focus and kick.*

The sea's warm, salty water turned icy cold. My kicking slowed. The back of my throat burned as more water forced its way into my mouth. Calves cramped and I had the sudden, uncontrollable urge to pee.

Overhead the moon's light winked out; I opened my mouth and swallowed the sea.

Soft hands slipped under my armpits. Fingers locked across my chest. Though the moon's light remained darkened, a new light emerged. Smaller, brighter, focused directly overhead.

Next moment I was gulping air, then coughing and hacking. More arms grabbed me. Someone rolled me onto my back. Flakes of snow stuck to my freezing-cold cheeks. I pried open my eyes; the effort took all my energy. An orange glow illuminated pine treetops. The roar of fire fueled by a cold wind competed with the honking of sirens and screams of my neighbors.

I was back home, back on the dock across from our apartment.

An EMT in a red jacket knelt over me, poking and prodding; another EMT shone a bright light into my eyes, blinding me. The light's brilliance clicked off. Slowly, very slowly through slits for eyes, my vision adjusted to the night. A crowd had gathered around me. Familiar faces stood behind the EMTs. Neighbors, mostly, but also …

… someone dressed in a cheerleading outfit. "Rog, don't you dare die! At least not until I get those study notes."

I wanted to reply to Becky Nance in my calmest, coolest, I'm really okay voice: "My study notes are in my book bag. And my book bag is in my bedroom, which at this point is pretty much toast." But of course I did not say this; I could not lift my head, could not open my mouth.

The EMT kneeling over me yelled, "Come on, kid, stay with us!"

"We're losing him!" came a second voice with more urgency.

Fists pounded my chest. The pain and pressure of probing and prodding diminished. So too did the beating on my sternum. The weight of bone and muscle, skin and tissue, lifted.

A jumble of warnings and pleas came rushing back to me: *You must decide if you will stay here on dis sea among deez islands where dere is buried treasure and beauty beyond belief … Forgive me, Ricky. Find me and forgive me before it's too late. … Please, Ricky, do not leave me.*

Somehow I found the strength to move my hand and finger the object in my pocket. At least I think I moved my hand. And the object I felt beneath the tips of my fingers was the pendant's ship wheel. Somehow I had brought it back with me—brought it back, but left the dog.

Which meant I had no choice but to return to pirate land.

CHAPTER 29

THIRD CHANCES, NEW ROMANCES

Stealing the *Black Avenger* proved easier than I would have imagined. Its crew remained ashore. LaFoote had not surfaced. Or if he had, I did not see him when I opened my eyes and found that I was no longer on the dock at home, as expected, but floating on my back. Kicking towards the great ship, I pulled Rebecca in my arms. Her hacking and coughing let me know she had not drowned. I had lots of questions about how I had ended up back with the pirates. I felt certain some of it would become clear with time, but right then we needed to get as far away from the pirates as possible.

There were cutlasses strewn about the ship in anticipation of the crew's return from the beach. I seized the biggest one and went to work, slashing through the anchor ropes until at last the cords parted. Slowly, the ship pivoted and pointed its bow toward the sea.

Upon hearing the anchor ropes splash, the crew on the beach realized their ship was leaving without them. They raced to the gigs, but with Rebecca's help, we dropped the topsail and a freshening breeze carried us out of reach of the gigs. While I steered us away from the island, Rebecca hurried below to free the Africans. If I were to captain the ship I would need all the help I could get.

Moments later men, women, boys, and girls gathered along the rail. When they saw the rest of the pirates in the gigs far behind us and realized that they were at last free, they shouted and cried. Sort of made me feel good, even though that was not my main reason for coming back. Helping Rebecca get to Port Charles, finding Dad, and saving the dog from the pirates: that's why I had returned. Plus, there was the promise of buried treasure. Find it and maybe Mom wouldn't have to keep driving trucks.

I showed Rebecca how to hold a course. Pointing to the compass, I said, "Keep it on a heading of 225. If the needle begins to move this way, turn the wheel that direction. If it starts to drift—"

"Have you ever sailed a dhow up the River Thames?"

"No."

"I have. One of the emissaries of the East India Trading Company had one built for the regattas off Tilbury. I was allowed to train on it for the summer. I *know* how to hold a course, Ricky Bradshaw. You need not worry about me."

But I was worried. I was worried I would lose her, again. Lose her forever.

We chased the clouds across a dark and stormy sky, sailing on a broad reach with a following sea. The *Black Avenger* sliced through the swells, moving away from Santa Maria. I had no doubt LaFoote would try to follow us in a stolen vessel. We had a substantial lead but would it be enough? And if he caught us, what then? The dog was gone, taken by Turtle Bill.

The doctor had warned that if I remained aboard the *Black Avenger* I would die: that the ship was cursed. Perhaps it was, but I pushed that thought away.

With one hand on the ship's wheel and my other arm wrapped around her waist, I stood beside her, listening to the heaving of the waves crashing against the ship's hull. The moon blazed bright above us. Her wild tangle of curls flew off her shoulders, the ends brittle and stiff from salt and wind. Bug bites marred her skin. A long laceration along her neck hinted at the struggle she'd had with Skinny Bob.

She leaned her head on my shoulder and sighed. "It's a three-day sail to my father's island. I have no idea how to find Port Charles. Do you?"

"There are charts in Doc's cabin. We'll figure it out."

Lightning flashed ahead of us. It was clear that in a few minutes we'd overtake the storm. Rain bounced off the binnacle, blurring the compass lens. Dark clouds were using up more of the sky.

"Will you remain in Port Charles?" Rebecca asked, her eyes pleading. "For a while, at least?"

"As long as I can."

It was as much as I could promise. What I could not explain to her, what she would never understand, was how I was on the *Black Avenger*. I was a lost soul in a world of pirates and buried treasure and stunning beauty. At any moment the paramedics on the dock might shock me back to life or jerk me out of my seizure. Or not. Could be this was my new reality.

With her hand cupped behind my head, she pulled my face close to hers and whispered, "Thank you." Her kiss was quick and wet and the perfect Christmas present.

And in that moment I knew there was no place I would have rather been than with her on a pirate ship sailing through the Caribbean.

Made in the USA
Middletown, DE
14 April 2020

88942975R00097